Victoria Marmot

and the

Shadow of Death

Virginia McClain

This is a work of fiction. Names, characters, businesses, governments, events, and incidents are the products of the author's imagination. Any resemblance to actual persons, living or dead, or actual events is purely coincidental.

Cover design by Natasha Snow

Works by Virginia McClain

The Victoria Marmot series:
Victoria Marmot and the Meddling Goddess
Victoria Marmot and the Inconvenient Prophecy
Victoria Marmot and the Shadow of Death
Victoria Marmot Book 4 is coming soon!

The Chronicles of Gensokai series:
Blade's Edge
Traitor's Hope

Short Stories
*Rain on a Summer's Afternoon**
*Note that you can get Rain on a Summer's Afternoon for free by subscribing to Virginia's newsletter

To Cedar, for being a shining light in the dark.

I WIPED THE sweat from my brow and tried, yet again, to roll the large block of granite up the side of the cliff, stopping it with my forehead when it finally reached head height, then lowering my wrists to lay against the boulder at my waist. My hands quivered, half with the strain of having pushed the block of granite into place, and half with trepidation. I took a deep breath, trying not to gag on the sulphur stench that permeated what passed for air here, and pulled my wrists as far apart as the manacles would allow. Then I pulled my forehead back, trying not to flinch. I really didn't want to graze myself again. The thumb on my left hand was still numb from the last time, and I was sincerely hoping that my efforts would pay off soon, because if I didn't get to a healer in the near future, I was pretty sure that gash was going to get infected.

The rock collided with the chain connecting the manacles, releasing an earsplitting crack that reverberated through the narrow canyon surrounding me. I almost cried as I felt my wrists fly outwards, the resistance from the steel chain that connected them finally giving way. Unfortunately, breaking the chain wouldn't restore my ability to pull myself through space and time, or to pull on my snow leopard form.

Throwing a suspicious glance at the brooding purple clouds that hovered in the thin strip of orange sky visible from my narrow prison, I scrambled onto the boulder in front of me and began the slightly less cumbersome process of beating the shit out of the shackles holding my ankles together. At least now I could aim the rock with my arms instead of my forehead.

Consequently, I didn't bash the crap out of my legs or ankles, or even tear up the skintight black jeans that had materialized the last time I'd shifted back into my human form (much to my dismay). Also, it meant it only took three good slams of the thirty-pound granite block against my ankle chains before they split.

Since my feet had been splayed as wide as they would go against the force of the chain, and now that force was removed, my legs went sprawling and I landed on my ass between the edge of the boulder and the cliff face. Luckily, I managed to drop the block away from me, so I wasn't pinned by anything. And I finally had four limbs free.

"Fuck yeah!" I shouted, dragging myself up so that I could stand on top of the boulder again and start climbing my way out of this cursed fucking canyon. No more worrying about drowning in the flash floods that swept through here every night. No more dodging rockfall, as whatever huge-assed creatures stampeding along the top of the canyon fled who the fuck knew what. And NO. MORE. GWENDAMNED. SQUIRREL. DEMONS.

I didn't care that half of my hand left hand was numb and useless, or that I hadn't eaten in days, or that I was pretty sure the water I'd drunk from the pools left behind by the flash floods had made me hallucinate. I was going to get the fuck out of this canyon, magic powers or no magic powers. Help or no help.

I still didn't know how I was going to get back to my own world after I got out of this canyon, but at least I wouldn't be stuck in a place that tried to kill me five times a day. At least I would be able to use my hands and feet.

I was extremely grateful that the canyon wall was riddled with handholds from all the broken rock that periodically tumbled to the bottom. Honestly, the place was surprisingly crumbly for a ravine carved out of granite. Generally that kind of thing was pretty stable, but… well, this wasn't even Earth, as far I could tell, so what the fuck did I know about how rocks should work here?

Anyway, I had no shortage of holds for climbing to the top of this thing. Which was a huge relief, considering that I had about three hundred feet to ascend before I reached the top, and falling would make for a pretty horrific death. I wasn't stoked about doing this without a rope at all, and with who knew how many unstable holds along the way. Especially considering how injured my left hand was. But my options were limited, and dying in a flash flood or getting crushed by rockfall really didn't appeal. Since those had clearly been likelihoods at the bottom of the canyon, I had little choice. I'd already shuffled for days in either direction to try to find a likely place to crush the bonds that held me, hoping that I might also get lucky enough to find a way out that didn't involve scaling one hundred meters of loose granite, but nothing had turned up except the literal rock and hard place I had used to break my chains.

I still didn't know what the damned things were made out of, but whatever it was, they kept me from pulling on the magic (or dark matter, or whatever you want to call it) that I normally had access to. Believe me, I'd tried, and I'd almost knocked myself out a few times over the past few days attempting to access my abilities in order to get out of this place. Especially after the damned squirrel showed up…

Of course, you're probably wondering how the hell I got here, and where the hell "here" is to begin with. The funny thing is: "hell" is my best guess for an answer at the moment. I really don't know where I am, except that MOME dropped me here when they finally got tired of Seamus' and my attempts to escape from the dungeon where they'd shoved us while I awaited my "trial." That's in quotes because I have no doubt that those asshats at MOME have about zero intention of giving me a fair trial. That was made evident on the very first day I regained consciousness in that shithole.

~~~
~~~

"*You're awake, Ms. Marmot. I'm impressed. I had rather expected to be trying a corpse.*"

I blinked into the light pouring out of what appeared to be a headlamp. The voice that addressed me was female and southern.

This particular southern accent was muted, and had that cloying condescension that comes from some educated southerners.

"*I've been told I'm full of surprises,*" *I muttered, still blinking, and wishing I could move my hands up to rub my eyes. My arms weren't restrained, but one of them was asleep from having been pinned underneath me for days and the other hurt so much whenever I tried to move it that it may as well have been a button labeled "to wish for death, press here.*"

"*You'll have to forgive me,*" *I continued, since I still couldn't see. "I'm not exactly up to speed on the who's who of douchecanoes employed by MOME. Do you have a name?*"

"*I was told you lacked manners, Ms. Marmot. I'm sad to discover it's true. However, since you've asked, I'm Rebecca Dryer, attorney at law and Magister in the High Courts of MOME.*"

"*Well, how very pretentious of you.*"

I had to admit, not being able to see the woman, despite all the light she'd brought down here, was starting to rub me the wrong way, and I was already irritable due to the whole trapped-in-a-cell-can't-move-half-my-body-feel-like-I'm-about-to-die scenario, as it was.

I had just now confirmed the trapped in a cell bit, though I had suspected it for a while now. But neither Seamus nor I had been able to see anything since we'd been in here, and the headlamp that Rebecca had brought with her provided our first illumination of the steel bars that separated us from the stone passageway in which she smugly stared at a clipboard.

I could finally see enough of her to make out the smugness and the clipboard.

She had curly hair. I couldn't really tell what color it was, because it was too short to fall in the direct beam of the headlamp, but something on the lighter side, I thought. And the rest of her features were too washed-out in shadows for me to be able to tell much about her. I didn't think it mattered. Whatever she looked like, I doubted she was here to trade fashion tips.

"Well, now that the niceties are taken care of," she said, blithely ignoring my quip about her pretentiousness, "Victoria Marmot, you stand accused of assaulting an officer of magical law enforcement with the intent to kill. How do you plead?"

"The fuck. What's going on?"

"You stand accused of——"

"I heard you the first time. What is going on here?"

"You are being tried for your crimes."

"Oh, that's rich. I bet it will be a fair trial and everything, too. Do I get representation? Do I even get to speak at this trial?"

"As I said, I had half expected to be trying a corpse. I'm sure that since you're conscious now, we can accommodate that. Now, please answer the question."

"Wait. You said that I stood accused of assault with intent to kill. That means he's not dead. The man I shot lived?"

"I am not allowed to share any details of this case with you. Your own magistrate will—"

"But you would sure as shit be trying me for murder if he'd died. So that means he's alive!"

"I can't say."

"You don't have to," I said, and I couldn't help it. I was smiling.

"You sound pleased," she said, after a pause.

"Look, that guy, whoever he was, is an asshole. But yeah. I'm glad he's not dead."

"Don't think it will reduce your sentence, simply because—"

"I don't care about the fucking sentence, lady. I'm glad he's not dead. I didn't want to kill him."

"Then why did you shoot him in the chest?"

"He was going to kill people I care about."

"Our officers only use deadly force in the most extreme circumstances. They would never harm an unarmed person who was in compliance with the law."

Seamus and I both laughed, though there wasn't humor in either of our tones.

"You tell yourself whatever you need to in order get to sleep at night, lady." I wasn't about to waste my breath convincing someone who was clearly going to be directly involved in whatever sham MOME had planned for my "trial" that MOME was the bad guy here.

"Listen here, young woman, you—a family member of a known convict, escapee from MOME's southern holding facilities, colluder with known criminals, and class A fugitive—shot a man in the chest just because he opened a door, before he'd had a chance to say anything to you. So don't you lecture me about sleeping at night."

That angered me enough that I almost tried to sit up, and the pain of it winded me for a moment. When I could speak again, it was very deliberate.

"Try this on for size. That known convict, also known as my brother, was abducted by masked men driving a fucking unmarked white van when we were eight years old. Those men worked for MOME. And why did they grab a terrified eight-year-old boy? Because they thought he might turn into something unsavory when he finally made his first change. Then, when my parents tried to get him back through the courts, MOME told my parents they were lucky MOME had "let" them keep me (who they would happily have snatched too if my mom hadn't physically fought them off). Then they pulled some bullshit to erase our memories and sent us packing. I spent my childhood thinking I was insane

because I remembered a brother that my parents didn't think existed. Turns out it was just that MOME's magic wasn't strong enough to erase him from his twin sister's memory. Of course, I didn't learn any of this until you assholes tried to meddle in my life AGAIN. Then, if memory serves, MOME followed me back to my home in Arizona in order to try to recapture my INNOCENT BROTHER, and in their attempts to do that they held my great-uncle's granddaughters HOSTAGE and tried to kill me and my friends. From there I've been stalked, beaten, and threatened by MOME operatives all over the world. So, yeah, when a MOME operative opened the door with a gun held to the head of my best friend's mother and started threatening me--which I'm pretty sure counts as talking by the way--I fucking shot him. In the chest. So he would drop the gun, and let everyone go, and not kill anybody I care about."

I took three deep breaths before I spoke again.

"So, I'm gonna go with not guilty, just on principle."

~~~

"I don't think you were supposed to say that kind of stuff without legal representation," Seamus said, after Rebecca Dryer was long gone.

I sighed. Seamus might have had a point.

"It's not like they were going to give me a fair trial, anyway. They're just going through the motions. If they don't,
~~~

they just give their opposition more ammo to use against them."

Rebecca Dryer had left without saying anything else, aside from asking me one or two questions about my injuries. Then she'd taken a minute to write a few things down on her clipboard. None of that had felt reassuring to me.

"Doesn't that mean that they have to give you a fair trial?" Seamus asked.

"No. It just has to look like one. I don't even know if the magical courts allow audiences, or what. Hell, all I even know about the U.S. legal system is from procedural crime shows. I'm talking out of my ass here."

Seamus chuckled. "Ew. Gross."

There wasn't much conviction in his voice, though.

Still, I started to laugh, and then tried to stop myself because the pain was too great.

"Are you feeling any better?" Seamus asked.

"I don't know. I'm not feeling any worse, but I still hurt all over. I'll let you know if anything stops hurting."

"It's a shame you're all beat up. This would be a great chance to have tons of sex."

"Seamus, stop making me laugh."

"I'm serious. It's pitch black, there's no one here, we have absolutely nothing else to do…"

"Seamus, cut it out. Laughing is excruciating."

"Well, if you need a distraction, you let me know."

"Seamus!"

The weird thing was, I totally agreed with him. It might have been the damned mating bond talking, but I couldn't help but feel like shagging would have been a much better way to spend our time.

"Oddly enough, I agree with you, but man, I hurt so much it cannot possibly be a good idea."

"To be clear, I'm not touching you with a ten-foot pole until you say you're all better and excited about sex. I am not into pain, certainly not your pain. I'm not suggesting we do anything. I'm just lamenting the missed opportunity."

He was silent for a moment.

"And now that I think about it, there's a good chance that's the mating bond talking, because honestly, I could have proposed that we write a new treatise on women's rights or something. I swear my brain wouldn't normally have jumped to sex."

"It's ok, Seamus, this mating bond thing is a jerk.... Besides, it would be kind of difficult to write a treatise on anything right now. For one thing, we don't have any paper. For another, it's pitch black in here. For another—"

Before I could finish, the sound of hinges screeching in the distance made both Seamus and me jump. I could tell Seamus jumped because the floor vibrated a bit. The sound of boots on stone rang out down the corridor, then more light flooded our cell.

"What the—"

"Victoria Marmot?" asked a voice in the darkness.

"Who's asking?"

I mean, because why the fuck not. I had nothing better to do, and talking was one of the few things that didn't hurt.

"Come to the cell door, please. We're here to check your injuries."

The voice was authoritative and masculine, but that did not add to the total fucks I had left to give.

"So, funny story: I'm not lying here for fun, asshole."

"Get up, please."

"I can't, genius. My injuries are such that moving is excruciating, I haven't even gotten close to trying to stand up without passing out. So, if you are here to look at my injuries, you can come and get it."

There was silence for a moment, then the light from the cell door passed over me and Seamus. I would have taken the chance to check out Seamus and make sure that he was ok, but I was still blinded by the light that had flashed my way. By the time I could see again, the light was focused elsewhere.

"Neutralize the other one."

"What? Wait! Don't hurt him!"

But before I was done talking, I heard the compressed air bang of a tranquilizer gun, a sound I was only familiar with thanks to my summers working in wildlife rescue. I was relieved and upset at the same time. Getting shot with a tranq was, by all accounts, no fun, but at least they hadn't done anything permanently damaging to him.

The cell door opened, and I tried to move so that I could see whoever was coming in, but the pain of adjusting my position was more than I could take and I almost passed out with the effort.

Before I could do any more, the light was shining in my eyes again and I couldn't see who was examining me, anyway. A set of hands started gently exploring the skin on my left side, and I couldn't help but flinch at the touch.

"She looks rough," said a second voice.

"Silence, Flemens," said the first voice that had spoken. The hands didn't waver in their assessment.

"What's the matter?" I asked. "Don't like the handiwork of your comrades? This is all courtesy of whichever MOME operatives came to pick me up at my home."

"Quiet, prisoner. No one asked you to talk."

"Funnily enough, I talk all the time without permission. You should try it sometime. It's very freeing. Might loosen that stick up your ass."

I might have imagined it, but I could have sworn I heard Flemens stifling a chuckle.

"Are you two here to finish the job your colleagues started? Not willing to risk me going to trial and telling the world what a corrupt organization of fascist douchetarts you have here?"

"I told you to be quiet."

"And I told you to pull the stick out of your ass. Oh wait. No I didn't. I just implied that. Sorry. Probably too subtle.

Let me try that again. You should really pull the stick out of your ass."

Silence, while the hands continued to gently prod what felt like every bruise I'd ever had in my entire existence come to life at once. The hands were professional and gentle, and I wondered if it was Flemens or StickAss examining me. Whoever it was, he was a consummate professional. I had to give him that. Still, the pain was so intense I had to talk to distract myself.

"So, which of you gentlemen is secretly questioning whether MOME is all that it has always pretended to be?" I asked. "Because I sure could use some help getting the hell out of here, and I don't particularly like the idea of being executed, or locked away for life, just for trying to defend the people I care about from a douchebag waving a gun around."

I was rambling, but I figured it couldn't hurt. After all, MOME seemed incredibly shady as soon as one took a look at it up close. I couldn't imagine how decent people managed to convince themselves that it was a fine place to work. Then again, maybe I could. People lied to themselves all the time, and I was sure that MOME worked hard to keep up a decent front, even on the inside. How many people even saw the authoritarian bullshit they pulled? Still, these two might have seen some of it, and one of them might even sympathize with me a bit. It couldn't hurt to push a few buttons.

"I mean, you can't seriously believe I wound up in this state because I fell down a flight of stairs or something, can you?"

"We were told you came to look like this because you shot one of our colleagues point-blank in the chest, then resisted arrest when they came to apprehend you."

"Sure, that's the story they would tell you."

"Are you saying that you didn't shoot Schreyer?"

"Is that his name? Schreyer? I definitely shot him, and I meant to shoot him. I didn't want *to kill him, but he left me with very few choices. I don't consider allowing someone to hold a gun to my best friend's mom's temple until they decide to pull the trigger a choice."*

"A MOME operative would never—"

"Shut it, Flemens. You don't know Schreyer. He would have."

Well, that was surprising. StickAss was on my side. At least for a half a second.

"And that is enough out of you, Ms. Marmot," StickAss said, just before I felt a sharp prick in my neck. "You should really rest."

~~~

When I came to, Seamus was sitting up, his back against a low, wireframe bed that was pushed up against the steel bars separating our cell from the next one over.
~~~

It took me a moment to realize how strange it was that I could see him.

"Who turned the lights on?" I asked.

The other strange thing was that I was lying on something soft, or at least, quite a bit softer than whatever I had been lying on for the past few days. And I was on my back, with my head turned to the side to look at Seamus. I turned it towards the ceiling and saw what looked like solid rock.

"Old school," I muttered, still too startled by finally being able to look at our surroundings to fully put together the strangest thing yet.

I turned my head to look at Seamus again, who was silently staring at his hands.

"Hey! That didn't hurt. Turning my head didn't hurt at all!"

I tried sitting up, and found that it was painless and simple. It was slightly more tiring than it ought to have been, but it didn't hurt at all. Something did feel strange about it, though—my right arm, back, and shoulder felt oddly tight. As though they were wrapped in plastic, or tape, or something. I was too excited about how little everything hurt to worry about it, though.

"Seamus, did those guys fix me up? I feel about a thousand times better than I did the last time we talked."

Seamus finally looked up from his hands.

"Yeah, Vic. They did everything they could to heal you, actually. I wasn't awake for it, after whatever they used to

knock me out, but they've come back to check on you a few times since then and filled me in a bit."

He didn't sound nearly as happy about this as I would have. I mean, damn. I had been worried that I was never going to walk again. The fact that I was no longer in pain, and that I could move all of my limbs easily and well… I was damned near giddy.

"Vic, I'm really sorry," Seamus said. My eyes snapped to his, and just to be sure he wasn't about to tell me I was paralyzed or something, I tried to stand up. It worked. My legs held my weight, and no part of me objected to the action of standing. Except for that tight pull across my skin.

"Why are you sorry?" I asked, now bewildered. My body worked. It didn't even feel as bad as it had after I'd torn my ACL and gotten surgery to replace the damned thing.

"You… umm… shit, why do I have to be the one to tell you this, when it's those MOME assholes who did this to you? Umm… take a look at your hands."

I looked down. My feet poked out from lime green pajama pants, which I could only assume were what passed for prison garb in the magical community. My feet looked like they always had. Dark, calloused, not particularly noteworthy in any regard.

I raised my hands up from my sides.

My left hand looked normal. The same caramel skin that had always covered it was there, all five digits present and mobile. Nothing out of the ordinary. My right hand…. Now

I could see why Seamus was sorry, although I couldn't say I was overly concerned. My right hand was covered in bright red scar tissue—the kind that comes from a third-degree burn. It encompassed 90 percent of my hand. Only my pointer finger and thumb appeared to be free of it. I turned my hands over and saw that I was missing three of my fingerprints. The hand moved well enough, aside from that tight feeling, but most of my original skin was gone. I followed the burn to the sleeve of my inmate pajamas and saw that it continued, so I pulled the sleeve up. It kept going.

I flexed my arm. I could feel the tightness all up and down my arm to my shoulder, along my shoulder blade, and back along my right side.

Not even glancing at Seamus, I pulled off the shirt and inspected my arm. The burn was everywhere I could feel tightness. It didn't cover much of the front of me other than the top of my shoulder. My chest was still my old skin. I tilted my head to look at my side, saw that it barely wrapped around to my rib cage at all, and in doing so I noticed the same tight pull on my neck. I ran my left hand along my neck, up to my ear and cheek. Slick scar all the way. It stopped about halfway up my right cheek.

"Huh," I said, taking a moment to register it all. "Is it all this same bright red?" I asked.

Seamus nodded, though I barely noticed the motion in my peripheral vision.

"They said it would take on a more natural tone with time. It's just red because it's new. They did everything they could to improve the… texture. Or that's what they told me, anyway."

I nodded. My left hand was still exploring all the new skin on my right side. It felt strange. Not just because the texture was so different from the rest of my skin, but because the sensation in the skin itself was weird. It felt partially numb, but also some of the feeling transferred to strange places. There were spots where touching the skin there made it feel like I was being touched six inches away, yet in many places the touch felt almost normal, albeit somewhat dulled. I couldn't stop touching it, but I was starting to get cold. I decided to put the long-sleeved lime green prison shirt back on, although my left hand instantly started exploring the skin of my right hand again.

"I'm so sorry, Vic."

Seamus sounded sincere. I just laughed.

"This might just be shock talking," I said, still feeling the skin on my right hand. "But I am so damned thankful that I can still walk that this really doesn't bother me."

I took a deep breath as I considered the thought that I would look… different for the rest of my life.

"That may change the more I think about it, but fuck, Seamus. I really thought I was going to be in pain for the rest of my life, and possibly immobile."

I looked up then, meeting Seamus' eyes, and he sat down on the bed behind me.

"Is it bad?" I asked, wondering how startling the facial scarring was. I didn't think I would care, but I'd be a little bit sad if Seamus and Sol didn't find me attractive anymore.

Seamus took a deep breath.

"You're still hot as fuck, if that's what you're asking."

His smile was so wide, I couldn't even accuse him of lying.

"Well, I'd like to pretend that I'm above caring what I look like, but I'm not sure I'm that zen. I don't know how I'll feel if I'm…"

If I'm what? I thought. Scars weren't necessarily ugly. They were just jarring, because they were usually a stark difference from what our brains expected to see when we looked at a person, and because they were very obvious signs of physical trauma. They were hard to ignore. I'd never worried about getting scars before. The scar from my knee surgery was a damned badge of honor, and despite my surgeons "suggestions" for keeping it from darkening in the sun, I showed that thing off at every opportunity. I had a few others left behind by various mishaps from childhood, some martial arts training incidents, running into a large metal door once, and I'd never worried about a single one of them. But this…

Burn scars were big, they could cover a lot of area, and they typically didn't ever heal fully. I mean, turn-back-into-normal-skin-heal… And this one certainly covered a large part of me. By rights, it still should have hurt like a son of a *bitch. The healing magic used on me must have bene pretty strong, if I was down to friendly red scar tissue at this point. Just judging by the size of the burn, it should have taken weeks to get this far.*

"Ugh… whatever," I sighed. "Surely we have more important things to worry about than whether or not I'm going to have a scar on my cheek for the rest of my life."

And I would, I realized, even as I said it. I would have a scar on my face forever…

Well, boo-fucking-hoo. I was just going to have to suck it up. I wasn't blowing smoke when I said I was happy to be fully mobile. The worry that I wouldn't be able to walk again had been real, and terrifying. The relief I felt at being able to move was like a physical weight being removed from my shoulders and chest. Sure, grieving my non-burned self was probably something it would be healthy to do at some point, but fuck it. Right now I really needed to focus on more important problems. Like how to not *get executed for shooting a guy who really deserved it.*

Seamus smiled and seemed to be reading my mind. "Right. So, how are we going to get you out of this?"

~~~

Of course, the answer was that we couldn't get me out of it. Despite five escape attempts and a
~~~

dozen stunned guards, nothing had gotten me out of the farce of a trial that awaited me. Yet.

It wasn't that MOME had us outmaneuvered, per se, it was just that they had us locked up where we couldn't use our magic, and they had finally stopped underestimating me now that I'd shot one of their agents, so the guards had all known how to fight hand to hand, and been armed, and… yeah. We never really stood a chance once they dragged us into that magic-blocking dungeon.

Except maybe if I could escape this hellscape and hotfoot it back to Earth without MOME knowing about it. That assumed that I could drag my ass to the top of this canyon without dying in some horrible and unforeseen fashion. Or any fashion, for that matter. Dying would really throw a wrench in my escape plans.

So, I took another deep, sulphur-laden breath, trying not to think about the pain in my hand, or how far I would fall if I missed a hold. Needless to say, I was embracing the "slow is smooth, and smooth is fast" method of climbing.

Keepin' it zen, that's me. Yep.

Right up until a shrieking squirrel demon leapt at my head, releasing the most terrifying series of squeaks and trills that I've ever had the misfortune to hear.

"AHHHHHHHHHH!" I screamed in return, trying desperately to grab onto the hold I'd just inadvertently jerked away from when the squirrel-thing leapt at my head. My first swipe missed, but, luckily, I hadn't thrown my body too wildly off-balance when I'd let go of the rock face, and had been moving up a portion of the cliff that sloped away from me, rather than towards me, so I had time to correct before I went toppling to my death. I managed to snag the hold I'd let go of on my second swipe, then promptly began cursing everything that had ever lived, but mostly the glowing-eyed, red-skinned, giant-fanged rodent that was now perched in front of my face, squealing with terror. Or maybe I was just terrified and projecting it back on the squirrel. It was hard to know.

"What. Do. You. WANT?!?" I said, trying to keep my own voice as level as possible. On some level I knew that freaking out was not going to help. After all, what creature ever responded well to being screamed at? But that was a difficult to impulse to control, especially after the number of times this creepy-assed gremlin had shown up and scared the hell out of me in the past week.

The only reply I got was, of course, more unintelligible screaming. Which was no surprise, as this creature had yet to produce any other sound in my presence.

I shrugged.

"Buddy, once again, I have no idea what you're trying to say, but I would really appreciate it if you could stop saying it with… so much volume and… enthusiasm?"

I wiped a fleck of squirrel demon spit from my chin to illustrate this last point.

Unlike everything else I'd ever said to the creature, that last bit seemed to garner some kind of understanding. The creature shifted its ears a bit flatter, cocked its head, and grabbed its own tail (the only part of it that sported any kind of fur) in a way that made me think it might be embarrassed.

Then it opened its mouth and screamed at me again.

"Ugh, dude, seriously. I'd rather have you spit at me than shriek like that. Anyway, I need to get to the top of this cliff without dying, so if you don't mind…" I made a slight shooing motion with my hand, to indicate that I wanted to move past the squirrel, and to my complete astonishment, it responded by moving out of my way.

Loath to lose my one chance at freedom from shrill noises, I resumed climbing, hoping to put as much distance between me and squirrel-thing as possible.

The three hours that it took me to make it to the top were so blissfully squirrel-demon-free that I'd largely forgotten the creature's existence by the time I launched myself, beached whale style, over the final ledge and lay, gasping and barely able to move through the exhaustion, at the top of the deep slot canyon that I had been trapped in for a week.

"Finally," said a high-pitched voice behind me. "I'm amazed you survived down there for so long, and I thought you'd never make it to the top climbing so slowly."

I turned, grunting with the effort of even that simple motion, after what was surely the longest unroped climb of my life, to see who the hell was talking to me.

I shit you not, it was the squirrel. The red-skinned, glowing-eyed, fluffy-tailed rodent-thing that had been tormenting me with its shrieking and random appearances for the past week was moving its mouth and forming words.

"Um… pardon my French, but… what the fuck?"

"That isn't French, kid."

"You can talk?"

The squirrel-thing nodded.

"With words?"

Now it glared.

"WITHOUT FUCKING SHRIEKING LIKE A BANSHEE?!"

And yeah, ok, I might have been mad enough that I sat up abruptly and shouted a bit, despite how tired I was.

"Hey! It's not my fault you couldn't understand me down there. That's the damned magic of the canyon. Or anti-magic, I guess. At any rate, I was talking to you just like now, but you could only hear shrieking."

"What?"

"In this realm there's a spell in place that lets most folks communicate, assuming they use a verbal language. But no spells work down in that canyon—it's an anti-magic void."

"How does that even work? I thought all magic was just dark matter anyway. How can you stop dark matter from working?"

"Beats me, kid. High energy fields, maybe? I dunno. I'm not a physicist or a mage, so… it's not really my thing."

"What are you, then?" I asked, before I could consider the fact that it might be rude to ask.

"Just a local," he replied, sounding a bit shifty.

"Uh huh… demon?" I hazarded.

He tilted his head again, this time locking me with just one glowing eye.

"You gonna run away screaming if I am?"

"Dude," I said, lying down again and staring at the creepy orange sky, finally able to see a good 180 degrees of it. "You are a talking, red-skinned, glowing-eyed squirrel-thing that almost made me fall off a cliff two hours ago. You really think finding out what you're called is going to make me run away?"

"Hmm… alright. Yeah. Folks from other realms call us demons sometimes, especially when they find us here. They sure as heck call us nicer things than that when we travel to *your* realm. Been called an angel more than once, myself."

I stared down one of his beady, glowing eyes, raising an eyebrow.

"What? You wait. If you saw me in *your* realm, you'd think I was quite the sight."

Too tired to argue, and fairly certain that I had no idea what I was talking about anyway, I shrugged.

"So, is this realm hell?" I asked.

Squirrel-thing nodded.

"One of 'em, yeah."

"What's your name?" I asked, not really wanting to get into how many hell realms there might be.

"Azrael."

That got another raised eyebrow.

"Azrael? Archangel of death, Azrael?"

Azrael shrugged.

"Maybe."

"You're a squirrel," I said.

"Squirrel, angel… same same," he shrugged.

"Why do you sound like you're from the south of London?"

"Last time I was in your realm, I spent a fair bit of time there."

"How do I get back to my realm from here?"

Azrael just stared at me for a moment.

"Same way you came in, Luv."

"I was dragged in by MOME agents against my will, through… what is it called again? A seam? I think."

Azrael nodded.

"That'd be it."

"You're telling me I can't leave unless I'm dragged out against my will by MOME agents?!"

"No, no. Nothing like that. But you have to leave by seam. It's the only way in or out of here."

"Well, how am I supposed to find it without my magic?" I asked.

"That would be difficult. Shouldn't matter now, though."

"What does that mean?" I sat up, no longer interested in the orange sky blotted with purple clouds. "Are you saying I have my magic again?"

I looked at my hands and feet, at the metal shackles that still encircled them.

"I didn't think breaking the chain would break whatever was keeping me from my magic. Are you telling me I didn't have to climb that freaking cliff? That I could have just shifted myself up here?!?"

"It wasn't the manacles that kept you from your magic, Luv. It was the canyon itself."

"But the MOME agent said—"

"Well, they're not exactly going to tell you how to escape, now, are they? Mind you, most people never manage to break those chains at all, let alone the manacles. And come to that, I've never seen anyone make it out of that canyon before, either."

I sighed and lay down for a second. I already knew I was too tired to shift myself any distance worth trying, so there was no point in making myself pass out.

"Probably because most people who wind up here grow up with magic," I mumbled.

"What's that?" Azrael hopped over so he was looking me in the eyes again, even though I was lying down.

"I grew up thinking I was a normal human. I've only had magic for a few days, or only known I've had it that long. It amounts to the same thing, anyway. Taking my magic away doesn't leave me as paralyzed as it might someone else. I'm used to having to make do with whatever my body is capable of."

"Whatchoo doin'?" asked Azrael, as my eyes started to close.

"Taking a nap," I mumbled. "Can't do shit if I pass out the first time I pull on my magic."

F COURSE AZRAEL waited until I'd just drifted off into a peaceful sleep before pouncing on my chest and batting my face with his tail repeatedly.

"Azrael. What the fuck?" I asked groggily, pawing his tail away from my face.

"There's a storm coming, and believe me when I tell you that you do NOT want to be out here when it hits."

I thought of all the flash floods in the bottom of the canyon, and also the sounds of large animals stampeding a few hours before each flood…

"Ok. I will take your word for that. So… where can I go? Is there high ground around here somewhere?"

Azrael shook his head.

"During a storm, the safest place in the realm is the bottom of that canyon."

"Fuck that. I am never going back down there. How do they expect any prisoners to survive down there? I mean, I assume they don't particularly care if I survive, but if you've seen other people stowed here…"

"They expect you to get washed down the canyon, I think. That's what happens to most of them, anyway. I think they have a collection unit at the bottom. Likely keeps most of them alive. I did try to tell you that on the first night."

That whole thought process, especially the bits in which I was supposed to have let myself get washed down the canyon, with my arms and legs shackled, no less, instead of resolutely climbing to high ground during each flood and eventually finding a way to break my manacles… it kind of made my blood boil.

I took a deep breath, deciding to let that go for now. I also ignored the idea that Azrael had been trying to impart useful information on the first night that he'd flown at me out of the darkness and started shrieking like a dying cat.

"So, what am I supposed to do, then? I don't have the energy to shift myself back to Earth from here. I'm exhausted."

"Luv, you could be as rested as the Queen on her birthday and you'd never be able to shift yourself to Earth from here. You'll have to find a seam. And you'd best get on with it, 'cause the storm will be here soon."

It did occur to me, briefly, to wonder what in the nine hells Azrael was getting out of this whole save-the-human-you'd-never-met-before-finding-her-randomly-at-the-bottom-of-a-canyon thing, but since it seemed likely that whatever nastiness these storms caused was just as likely to kill a squirrel-sized demon as a 150lb human, I decided it didn't really require that much assessment. He was probably just trying to save his own ass.

"So, how do I find a seam?" I asked, eyeing the angrier-looking purple clouds above us, which were beginning to blot out the orange sky.

"How does a dragon not know how to find a seam?"

Azrael's voice was so incredulous that I actually turned to look at him. His face showed as much indignance as I thought was possible from a squirrel, demon or not.

"I don't know what I look like to you, buddy, but I'm not a dragon."

I could feel my eyebrows reaching for my hairline, but Azrael skittered back from me and started gesturing wildly to the ground behind me.

"Have you never seen your Shadow?" he asked.

"Umm… I have, on more than one occasion, looked at the silhouette of my body cast by the sun. I have a feeling that's not what you're talking about, though."

"That's exactly what I'm talking about, Luv, but on this planet the sun doesn't just shine a tiny portion of the electromagnetic spectrum through the atmosphere, and the creatures here are built to actually *see* things properly. Look."

He gestured emphatically at the ground behind me.

I turned to look, but only saw an even darkness spread on the ground.

"Shit," Azrael mumbled. "The cloud cover is too dark, and you'd probably have to call on your snow leopard to see it anyway, but believe you me, your Shadow tells the whole story."

I found it both suspicious and creepy that Azrael knew I had a snow leopard form, and it irked me that there was something different about the shadows here that I wasn't catching. I tried looking at the ground behind Azrael, but I only saw the general darkness cast by the clouds in the sky.

"Never mind," he muttered. "No point now. And you already said you were raised without magic, so I don't know why I'm surprised. Look, just close your eyes and feel around for a break in the ether."

That was a sentence that would have made less than zero sense to me even a week ago, but, weirdly enough, thanks to the crazy turn my life had taken lately, I actually had some sense of what he was talking about.

I closed my eyes, centered my breathing the way I did at the beginning of a training session, and tried to sense any gaps in the energy that surrounded me.

I felt for a rift in the darkness, seeking for the seam. Just as I found an edge between the energy that suffused the world and the nothing between it, I felt something warm and slick stick to my leg. Without waiting to find out what the hell it was, and hoping desperately I would still have a leg on the other side, I pulled.

I WAS BLINDED by a white light and felt the sweep of large wings as I fell backwards against cold, hard rock. By the time my eyes had adjusted to the dim glow of the light around me, whatever had blinded me was long gone. The only thing left was…

"Seamus?"

"Vic?!? Is that really you? They tried to tell me you were dead."

"What? Who tried to—Gwendamn it!"

And that was when I realized I was right back in the same fucking dungeon I'd started out in before they'd shipped me off to solitary. I tried to pull on my snow leopard form, my Gwen-given powers, anything. Nothing worked. I was right back where I'd started. F. M. L.

~~~
~~~

The next day, after a long night of banging my head against the wall, cursing myself, Azrael, and MOME, Seamus and I were both dragged out of our cell and through multiple rock corridors, finally reaching a bland, drywall-covered maze that led us from one shitty, neon hellhole to the next, until we emerged into a grand marble foyer opening onto a set of large, arched wooden doors.

Beyond the wooden doors lay a round room encircled by high benches laden with people in robes. Great. I felt like I'd walked into the Wizengamot or some shit. If I saw Dolores Umbridge holding a gavel, I was going to lose my shit.

"You ever been to this kind of thing before?" I whispered to Seamus, who had his hands tied behind his back, just like I did, and who was being manhandled through the room right behind me.

"Nope. Wolf justice… looks different," he whispered back.

"Silence!" That was a voice from somewhere in the darkness that surrounded the circle we'd finally stopped in.

The center of the circle was brightly lit, while the benches surrounding it were dark, leaving us blind to everything but the otherwise empty space we inhabited.

"Lovely set up you have here. I was really digging the antique bleachers. Shame we can't see them anymore."

Apparently, I fought my spiraling fear of death or incarceration with sass.

"I said, silence!"

"Yeah. I heard you the first time. Did no one else mention that I'm terrible with following orders? I'm surprised it didn't come up. The lawyer I talked to found it fairly irksome, and the medics drugged me to stop me from talking. Oh, and you guys threw me into a hell dimension just to keep me out of your hair for a while, so—"

"Siopí!" shouted the voice in the darkness. I felt a slight buzz pass over my skin, and wondered if that meant someone had just cast a spell.

"Is that Greek? Cool! I didn't know that Arizona had much of a Greek population."

Much muttering and gasping followed that exclamation.

"Are you all Greek? Did I just offend you all? I can't see shit past this circle of light, you know, so you'll have to forgive me if I've missed some visual cues."

Seamus snickered behind me.

"What?" I asked.

"I think that was supposed to be a spell to make you shut up."

"And it didn't work?" I asked.

He chuckled again.

"Well, I can still hear you. I'm guessing they can too."

I turned back to the darkness around us, in the general direction of the voice that had uttered the spell.

"I told you, I really don't take orders well. I thought I was supposed to testify, though. I can't do that if I've been silenced." Not that I actually expected to be allowed to testify—I fully expected them to conveniently "forget" about that part—but if they were going to pretend this was a trial, then I was going to keep reminding them of it. Not for the first time, I wished that lawyer had left behind a book on mage law or something.

"You will be quiet, or you will be removed from this court."

"Now that seems counterintuitive. I'm here so that you can ask me questions. Kicking me out for talking would just be silly. That would be hard to explain to your dissenters, wouldn't it? Are there any reporters here?"

That caused another stir, and sure enough, no one repeated the threat. I supposed I'd guessed right about the reporters and the dissenters. I guess they had to at least make it *look* like a fair trial.

"So, now that you've dragged us all the way up here, what did you want to know?" I wasn't feeling at all cooperative, but I at least wanted to get this farce over with. I knew that silence wouldn't help me, but giving the mages time to compose themselves didn't help me either.

"How long have you been working with the Openers?" The question came from a different voice than the one that had been telling me to shut up in Greek.

"That doesn't sound like a formal inquiry, that sounds more like an interrogation. Is this an interrogation? Weird."

"Answer the question!"

"Sure, but hey, is this being recorded? I want a record of this whole trial. Do you mages have anything close enough to due process to grant that, or are you just going to report whatever you like when this is all over?"

"The trial is being recorded. Now answer the question."

"But who has access to the recording? And can it be altered? Honestly, I would feel more comfortable if someone I knew were here, or at least privy to the recordings."

"You are allowed to request a witness," said a third voice.

"Great. How about Albert Bumblebee?"

I had been thinking about it since my first talk with Rebecca Dryer. Of course, I'd been a bit distracted since then, but as soon as I found myself trapped here again last night, I'd decided that the best person to ask for was my high school principal. Naturally, I would rather have requested my brother, or Sol, or anyone else I actually knew well, but all the people I was closest to were wanted by MOME, and none of them could show up on my behalf without getting locked up themselves. To my knowledge, Albert Bumblebee was free and clear with this court, and also a mage. He seemed to like me, and had tried to help me a couple of times already.

"What is your association with Grand Master Bumblebee?"

"Grand Master?" That was news to me. "Albert's my homie," I said, delighting in the consternation that seemed to be coming from the bleachers. "He's also my school principal."

"You will address Grand Master Bumblebee with the appropriate respect!" demanded a furious voice on the other side of the darkness.

"She is addressing me just as I requested she address me, Master Elfthwin," came a familiar voice from behind me.

Sure enough, a few more seconds produced the unmistakable smell of pot smoke and patchouli that marked the presence of my high school principal.

"Hey Al," I said, as I felt the old man's hand pat my shoulder reassuringly.

"Sorry I'm late," he said. "I got here as quickly as I could."

I just stared at him for a moment.

"Considering I only asked for you about ninety seconds ago, I'd say you were plenty quick."

Albert looked somewhat offended, but before I could ask how on earth I'd managed to insult him, one of the voices from the darkness called for order.

Albert peered into the darkness, then clucked his tongue.

"No, this won't do at all," he muttered. Then he reached inside his robe, pulled out a joint, put it back in his robe, then pulled out a wand and waved it in a circle around us.

Suddenly the entire chamber was lit evenly, and we could see everyone in the bleachers that surrounded us.

"Ugh," I said. "I think I liked it better when we couldn't see everyone."

Albert chuckled, as did Seamus. I was only half joking.

It wasn't like we were surrounded by rows and rows of sea slugs or anything. Everyone in the bleachers looked pretty normal, outside of the fact that they were dressed like a university convocation ceremony, it was just that… well, it was easier to laugh off a room full of people who were hostile towards you when they were just a bunch of angry voices in the dark than it was when you could make eye contact with them and sense their very real hatred for you.

"Grand Master Bumblebee, may we ask why you've chosen to act as witness for this… criminal?" That was a middle-aged looking man wearing a particularly odd hat, which I supposed could have been a symbol of leadership… I mean, I would have expected it to be the symbol of leadership at say… clown school.

"Oh, but I haven't," Albert replied, causing my brain to stutter for a moment, as I wondered if Albert was about to feed me to the proverbial wolves.

"Did you not come here at the behest of Ms. Marmot, to act as her witness?" the man wearing the lead clown hat asked.

"No."

My stomach sank further, each time Albert spoke.

"Then why are you here?"

"I'm here as Ms. Marmot's legal representation."

~~~

After I managed to pick my jaw up off the floor, the trial proceeded... differently than I had expected. Honestly, when I'd requested Albert Bumblebee as my witness, it had simply been because I'd expected him to be my best shot at having a mage who wouldn't ruffle too many feathers in the court show up, and possibly give an honest account of whatever happened to my brother and Sol.

I hadn't even known what the official obligations of a witness were, or that Albert Bumblebee might in any way be some sort of grand poobah in the mage world. I honestly wasn't even sure the dude would be of any use, or on my side. All his previous affiliation with MOME might have hurt more than helped, and I wasn't 100% sure I could trust him. He had been the best of a lot of bad options.

So, when it turned out that he not only commanded the respect of every mage in that courtroom, but also knew the legal system as well as he
~~~

knew his own pipe collection… let's just say I enjoyed the hell out of watching the rest of the room squirm while they tried their damndest to accuse me of wrongdoing without offending my defense attorney.

And, boy, did he slay as my attorney.

Rebecca Dryer didn't stand a chance, though she sputtered and argued a lot anyway, glaring at Albert with the kind of venom one generally reserves for lifelong enemies and supporters of rival sports teams.

I had entered that courtroom hoping that they wouldn't decide to execute me, or that they would at least spare Seamus, if they were going to kill me anyway. My distant hope was that they would sentence me to something possibly escapable, like life imprisonment.

I walked out of there free to go wherever I wanted, along with both Albert and Seamus.

"Well, that was unexpected," I said, as we stepped out of the courtroom into the large marble foyer.

"Was it?" Albert asked. "I'm sorry, dear, I should have sent word that I was coming. There are some useful rats in this place that could certainly have delivered a message, if I'd thought of it. Sorry to leave you expecting the worst."

I shrugged, unsure if Albert meant literal or figurative rats, and not really wanting to think about it too much, either way.

Albert pulled out the joint he'd accidentally removed when he was looking for his wand earlier, and lit it.

"Though I suppose that would have taken some of the dramatic flair from my entrance," he said, as he finally exhaled a lungful of pot smoke.

He offered me the joint with a gesture, but I shook my head. It was damned tempting, after the week I'd had, but… well, after just narrowly escaping life in prison, breaking any law at all was less than appealing. He offered it to Seamus, who just stood there looking awkward for a moment before mumbling, "No, thanks."

"There's no smoking in this building, Cynthia," came a voice from behind me.

I turned to see Rebecca Dryer, the prosecuting attorney, or magistrate, or whatever the hell mage lawyers called themselves, glaring at the three of us.

Albert waved the joint in her direction in a silent greeting.

"Still smarting from your loss, Becks?"

"Fuck off, Cynthia."

"Come now, there's no need to be rude, Rebecca. What will the children think?"

"I don't care what you and your criminal brood think. Get off the damned premises, if you're going to waste your breath on that thrice-cursed human brain candy."

"You should really try it sometime, Becks. Delightful substance, keeps the vamps away—not that you've ever minded the creepy diamond skulls. Might help you relax."

"Oh… sit on it and spin, bitch."

And with that, Rebecca Dryer stormed out of the foyer through one of the three metal doors that led to the neon-lit maze beyond.

"Did she just call you Cynthia?" I asked, not sure what part of that exchange had confused me the most.

"She really has never gotten over the way we treated each other as school girls," Albert said.

"Oh… right." I mumbled, realization slowly dawning. "Well, shitty of her not to call you by your real name, though. That's a stupidly low thing to do."

Albert nodded appreciatively, foot-long white beard brushing his chest all the while, then shrugged.

"Of course, she would argue that Cynthia *is* my real name…. Honestly, if it makes her feel better, I won't hold it against her," Albert said, as we moved towards one of the other metal doors. "Life is too short, and all of that. Besides, I was rather mean to her in school."

Albert pushed open the farthest right of the three doors, and gestured for us to lead the way.

"Shall we be off, then?" he asked.

I had no idea where we were going, but I nodded, and, as Seamus didn't say anything behind me, I could only imagine that he did the same.

Albert grabbed both of our elbows, then the world winked out.

I SUPPOSE I shouldn't have been surprised to find myself standing in the middle of the Andes, on a hillside that was far too cold for my black leather jacket and skintight black jeans.

"Seriously, I need to talk to Gwen about this clothing thing. These boots are solid enough, but why do they need a three-inch heel? And why can't I ever be wearing a parka when we show up in the Andes?"

"I thought your clothes only changed when you shifted from snow leopard to human?" Seamus said, eyeing my outfit suspiciously.

"I thought so too, but that's the third time my clothes have changed just when I've shifted location… and they haven't even been location appropriate. I honestly think it's just that Gwen likes leather."

Seamus swept his amber eyes over my body and smiled.

"It does suit you," he said.

"Yeah, well, it's fucking cold."

I grabbed his arm and pulled him towards me.

"Now you have to cuddle me for warmth," I muttered, burying my face in his shoulder.

What I wouldn't tell anyone, for any amount of money, was how close I was to tears just seeing Seamus eye me with that much longing in his eyes, despite the burn on my face.

I still hadn't seen the damn thing in a mirror, and I'd almost forgotten it even existed, what with the whole life on trial thing happening, but... ugh. Vanity was stupid.

"What happened to consent?" he asked, even as he wrapped his arms around me.

"You said you liked being touchy-feely with your friends," I said. "But you're right, I totally should have asked."

I snuggled closer and he held me tighter. I would be sure to ask next time.

"Now then, you love birds, we need to get to that blasted cabin."

I had almost forgotten Albert was there.

"Right. Down the hill about a kilometer. Do you have some kind of magey way of traveling quickly?

It would be easier for us to shift to animal form and run there, but I don't want to abandon you."

Albert smiled.

"I have my ways. After you, Victoria."

I shuddered.

"Please, Albert, call me Vic."

He frowned, then nodded.

"Of course. I'm sorry. I didn't realize that you don't like your full name."

I shrugged, then closed my eyes and imagined what it felt like to be covered in warm fur, racing on four legs down a mountainside. Then, in a moment of awesomeness that I didn't think I would ever get used to, I *was* covered in fur and racing down a mountainside on four legs.

Suddenly, all else was forgotten. Scars, MOME trials, dungeons, cryptic messages left by my parents, escaping a hell realm, none of it mattered. All that mattered was me and the rocks beneath my paws, the balance my tail provided as I skittered down cliff sides, and the clean scent of snow and pines on the breeze, lightly tinged with squirrel.

Before I knew what I was doing, I was veering away from where I could smell the smoke of Sol's cabin, off into a patch of low boulders and scrub oak to my right, which I was now certain housed a small, fat rodent.

My mouth watered, and it finally sank in that I had barely eaten in the past week. They hadn't even offered me a meal before my trial, and food had been more than scarce in the canyon that I'd been trapped in within the hell realm.

I slunk across the rocks, my profile lowered, my nose probing the air to ensure that I was downwind of my prey.

I ignored the howl I heard in the distance, zeroing in on the tiny heart I could somehow hear beating a few meters away. I might have drooled. I wasn't sure. I felt my tongue reflexively clean my lips, at any rate.

A part of my brain recoiled at the vision of my large canines piercing the flesh of some poor defenseless rodent, but most of me was too hungry to care. Besides, even though I was vegetarian in my human form, I had nothing against a snow leopard catching its dinner. Even if that snow leopard was me.

I checked my footing on the snowy, rocky hillside, readying my muscles to pounce onto the hole that I now knew contained the squirrel. One more deep breath, and…

Light brighter than the midday sun now filling the sky flashed in front of me, and I lost all sense of time and space as I scuttled backwards, my feline reflexes just barely keeping me upright as I let out a yowl of consternation.

"I do not appreciate becoming supper, Luv," said a deep voice, which rang a small bell of familiarity in my mind.

I blinked repeatedly, and soon found myself assuming human form around the words, "Do I know you?"

"Damn. What kind of shifter doesn't show up naked after they shift? Poor form, Luv. I was really looking forward to that."

The figure in front of me looked like nothing I'd ever seen before. Actually, that wasn't entirely true. He looked a bit like Rhelia, with the smoothest, darkest ebony skin I'd ever seen, minus the iridescence and plus a pair of giant silver wings.

It took me a minute before my brain stumbled forward with an answer.

"Azrael? Squirrel demon? Is that really you? Were you the squirrel I was about to eat?"

It didn't exactly make sense, but it was the only thing I could come up with.

"In the flesh. Told you I was an angel, Luv. Everyone in this realm loves me."

Something about the way he said it sounded a bit forced.

"Really?" I hazarded. "Everyone loves the arch-angel of death?"

He shrugged, his handsome features catching the light in a way that made my breath hitch.

"That's all just a misunderstanding, really, and I can tell you're already warming up to me," he said, dropping a wink at me that made my stomach drop a bit. There was something decidedly… compelling about him. And not just because he was the most handsome person I'd ever met.

Then I felt fur in my hand, heard a soft growl, and looked down to see a brief flash of black wolf before Seamus stood beside me. He looked… awed.

"Who is this?" he asked.

"This is Azrael. He's… a friend."

I watched Seamus' expression turn from awe to puzzlement, then back to awe.

"He?" he asked.

I was about to gesture at the very obviously masculine body of the winged creature in front of us— I mean, hell, Azrael was basically wearing a loin cloth. He was chest to the wind, and so obviously male that I actually gasped in shock when I turned back to look at him and saw a person with the same gorgeous features, but instead of a masculinely sculpted set of pectorals she had a set of breasts almost as perfect as Sol's, a slender but athletic waist… everything about her was still muscular, sculpted, beautiful, but now it was all decidedly female.

"Umm…"

Azrael laughed.

"Oh, how delightful, Luv—you're a bridge! One of the lucky few who get to see both of me."

I tried to shut my mouth before I spat out something overly honest, like the fact that I couldn't decide which Azrael was sexier, or the fact that I shouldn't be thinking that either of them was sexy, since we had more important things to think about at the moment, or… yeah. It was really best to keep my mouth shut. Luckily, Seamus seemed to be feeling talkative.

"What do you mean, both of you?" he asked.

"Vic here, as a being who is equally attracted to men and women, can see both aspects of my angel form. Most folks only see one or the other, even if they have some leanings in both directions. Not very many folks find themselves with an even split, and whichever sex they find most attractive is what they see when they look at me. You, for example, will only ever see me as a female. That angry woman, down the hill there, will only ever see me as a woman. But Vic, bless her, will see me as whatever the nearest person fancies, or maybe even see both of me at once, sometimes. That can be a bit confusing for folks."

I was intensely curious about what Azrael was saying, but his comment about the angry woman down the hill had me turning around just in time to see Sol shift to her panther form and come bounding up the hill.

"**W**HERE THE FUCK have you two BEEN!?!" Sol shouted, once she'd taken a moment to resume her human form and take her eyes off of Azrael's almost-naked body.

"Albert didn't tell you?" I asked.

"No one has told us shit since Gwen abandoned us here a week and a half ago!"

"Well, don't yell at me, I've been locked up in a dungeon and a hell dimension," I said, raising my hands.

"Me too," said Seamus, similarly raising his hands in the universal sign for *please don't rip my head off*. "Well, not the hell dimension, but still."

Sol looked about ready to punch something, but then she looked back at me and did a double take.

I almost flinched when she reached for me, but she instantly wrapped me in her arms and was kissing both of my cheeks, eyelids.

"Damn it, Gatita. I was fucking worried. What happened to you?"

I knew that she meant my scar. I mean, I'm sure she meant my general well-being too, but… I could tell it was the scar that had turned her from righteous ire to concern.

"What do you think happened?" I asked, caught between wanting more of her kisses and wanting to push her away from the skin on my body that still transferred sensation so oddly.

"I will kill the MOME bastard responsible for this," she muttered into my hair, pulling me closer.

"Ah, reunited at last, I see," said a British voice, quite different from the one that had been explaining its dual sex from a nearby boulder only a moment before.

"Albert," I said, looking up from Sol's shoulder, "this is—"

But as I turned to introduce Albert to Azrael, I saw a whole lotta open sky where there should have been an angel, or a least a fucking squirrel.

"Where the fuck did they go?" I muttered.

"Who, Gatita?" Sol asked, pulling back to look at me again.

"Seamus, I didn't imagine the whole angel thing, did I?"

Seamus smiled and shook his head, stepping closer and nudging Sol with his shoulder.

"Can I get a hug too?" he asked.

After Sol wrapped him in a slightly begrudging embrace, he turned to me.

"No, Vic. That gorgeous winged creature was real. Or… if she wasn't, she was a group hallucination."

I sighed.

"I can't believe the shrieking squirrel demon is a Gwendamned angel."

"Angel—" Albert began, just as a new voice asked, "Who am I damning?"

"Oh great." I laughed. "The party's all here."

~~~

I wasn't expecting to burst into tears when I hugged Trev for the first time after getting away from that MOME dungeon, but what can I say? Trev, running at me with his own eyes full of saline, was more than my emotionally beleaguered, sleep-deprived self could handle, and as soon as his arms wrapped around me we became an indistinguishable mass of damp, salty human.
~~~

"Thank gods you're alive," Trev muttered, as we laughed and hugged in a more desperate fashion than a week's separation probably warranted, but damned if it didn't feel like longer somehow. I suppose getting captured by the oppressive regime that's trying to kill you and your whole family/everyone that you love will do that to a person.

Eventually we broke apart and turned to find everyone standing behind us looking a bit glassy-eyed.

"Ok. Gushy reunions over. What'd I miss?"

THE ANSWER WAS, not much, as it happened. After everyone filed back into Sol's cabin and settled into the comfortable couches and chairs that filled up the cozy living room around the delightful wood stove, we swapped tales of all that had happened in the past ten days.

I had suffered the more "exciting" week-and-a-half by far. I had been hit by a lethal spell, arrested, and locked away in a hell dimension until my trial. Everyone else had just been looking for my mom's journals, without much success.

"So… with the Flagstaff house a pile of cinders, where do we look next?" I asked, trying not to let emotion clog my throat. I still hadn't recovered from the shock of learning that particular detail during the trial—of course, MOME hadn't even had the decency to explain how it had happened, they had just claimed that the house had unexpectedly burned down while I was being held.

Seamus and Sol looked questioningly between Trev and me, while Albert sat in considerate silence. I suppose it made sense that neither Sol nor Seamus would have suggestions. They'd never even met my parents, let alone known them well enough to have an idea where they might hide something incredibly valuable. Albert seemed like he might have reason to know what my parents would have done with these mysterious journals, but he remained mum.

Trev just stared at me in silence.

"We have to go back to the house in Colorado, don't we?" I asked.

Trev nodded slowly.

"Vic, you don't have to go if you don't want to. I never lived at the house in Colorado. I can search it and—"

"No, it's fine. I can think of a few places worth looking that you might not think of, or know about. And besides, it seems like the next stretch of my life is just going to be reminder after reminder that Mom and Dad are gone. Not to mention that they weren't who I always thought they were. It can't hurt to start confronting the memories now."

"It could, actually," Sol said, much to my surprise.

When I turned and met her eyes, she looked more haunted than I'd ever seen her.

"I don't mean you shouldn't do it," she clarified. "Only that it might hurt a fair bit, really, when the time comes."

"That's not what I—gods, why have I been so self-absorbed in the past few weeks that I've been acting like I'm the only person in the world who's ever lost someone? You and Seamus have both clearly been fighting some of your own demons, and I haven't even taken the time to ask what the hell is going on."

Sol gave a lopsided smile and said, "Well, if I recall correctly, the last time we spent more than a few minutes in each other's company, none of us were particularly interested in talking. I don't think that's your fault, Gatita."

Seamus chuckled. "And it's not as though we've had much time to discuss anything since then. We keep getting chased off by MOME before we even have five minutes to get comfortable together."

"Speaking of which," I began, taking a good look around the room for a minute, "why is it that we trust that MOME hasn't covered this place with bugs, or whatever the magical equivalent is? Not to mention, why aren't they blowing the place up, or knocking the door down trying to get to us? It's not like they don't know where it is."

"Fair question," said a voice from the doorway.

I swear all of us were up and getting ready to fight before Gwen even took a full step away from the door.

"Damn it, Gwen! Don't sneak up on people like that. Also, what the hell? I thought you were already here, why are you lurking in the doorway?"

The smirk on the red-haired goddess' face made me want to slap her, but I refrained.

"But your question is a good one," she replied using impressively selective hearing. "As it happens, I know the answer to this one. I thought you would be pleased."

I sighed, sitting back down on the couch, where I had been comfortably resting my legs in Seamus' lap and my head in Sol's. Everyone else followed suit, and Gwen glided her way further into the cabin.

"After all of you took off on your last adventure and MOME was left here with a partially smoldering log cabin, Sol's grandmother showed up to fight the fire and save what she could of the property. Luckily, MOME lost interest in the place as soon as they confirmed that no one was left inside.

As I found myself in the area while Sol's family worked to save the place, I was able to help. Further, after the fire was put out and the damage repaired, I helped to put some illusions in place to make MOME think that the place burned to the ground after they left, and is consequently of little interest."

Knowing what Gwen was capable of in terms of disguise, not to mention in terms of… being a goddess, I didn't doubt that she'd done a very convincing job of it.

"So, thanks for that," I said, not wanting to sound too ungrateful. "But why are you here now?"

I was always a bit wary of Gwen. Her heart was in the right place, but she had a funny way of "helping" people sometimes.

"Two things, really. One, to check in on how your quest is going, and two, to find out why you decided to bring Azrael, Devourer of Souls, back into the mortal realm."

E VERYONE STARED ACCUSINGLY at me, while I stared slack-jawed at Gwen.

"Azrael is the Devourer of Souls?" I asked, somewhat incredulous.

Gwen nodded.

"That… shrieking squirrel demon thing is… the Devourer of Souls?"

"More *a* devourer of souls—they're really a succubus. Or, at least, that's another name for them, anyway. I suppose they're rather hard to categorize, when you get down to it, but so are most demons, come to that—when you look at them from a perspective other than the monotheists-rewrite-history-to-suit-themselves one. The hell realms are fascinating, when you learn to see past the—"

"So, I didn't kick off the apocalypse or anything, by letting Azrael hitch a ride?" I interrupted, before Gwen could get too caught up in… whatever it was she was about to ramble on about. Probably some "explanation" about how things worked that would inevitably leave me with another million questions about how everything actually worked.

"Hardly! They are awfully frisky, but scarcely about to take out the entire earth singlehandedly," Gwen admitted.

"I'm confused," Trev muttered, while Sol nodded and Seamus smiled nostalgically, in all likelihood remembering the angelic version of Azrael he'd met earlier.

"Azrael sort of helped me escape the hell dimension I was stuck in," I said.

"Sort of?" Sol asked.

"Well, they explained a few things that were clutch in terms of getting out."

"And then they conveniently hitched a ride?" Albert asked, speaking for the first time since we'd entered the cabin.

"Well… yeah. I didn't think anything of it, at the time. It didn't seem like a great place to be stuck, even for demonic squirrel-thing… is it a big deal that they're here?"

Albert shrugged.

"I can think of a few people who will be less than pleased that they're here. I, for one, look forward to seeing them around."

The raising and lowering of bushy white eyebrows that followed this statement left little doubt as to why Albert would be pleased to see Azrael.

"Is there anyone they *don't* try to seduce?" I asked, before I could think better of it.

"Oh certainly! And beware if Azrael ever truly attempts to do more than flirt, Vic. They are called a Devourer of Souls for a reason. They don't *have* to take all of your soul, but they certainly can, if they feel like it."

That certainly took a bit of the shine off of Azrael's sex appeal.

"So… did I answer your question, Gwen?" I said, turning back to Gwen. Only to find her gone. Because, of course she was.

"She didn't even pretend to stick around and ask how my quest was going?" I muttered.

"Cheer up," said Seamus, patting my leg with exaggerated good humor. "We have no idea how long she was lurking around while we were talking. She may have heard everything already, and only interrupted when it didn't seem likely that you were going to bring up Azrael on your own."

Somehow I didn't find that comforting at all.

I LOOKED AT the mountains that loomed before us, taking up more than half the horizon to the west, inhaled the crisp, autumnal, mountain air… and suddenly felt transported through time. I could almost hear my parents' laughter on the wind. Could smell the pine forests that we'd escaped to so often when my school schedule hadn't allowed us to travel farther afield.

"Damn it."

"What is it?" asked Sol.

"We're not even at the house yet, and I'm getting choked up just breathing the air here."

My eyes were full of tears, and I wiped at them, not out of shame, but out of a desperate need to not feel this much pain. This was a big part of why I had leapt at the chance to move into the house in

Flagstaff. Everything in this damned state reminded me of my parents, in some way or another.

"It changes," Sol said, after a long silence in which we'd both just stood staring at the mountains. "People say it gets easier, but that hasn't been my experience, really. It just… happens less often. That feeling that you've been punched in the gut and then hollowed out from the inside… it still hits me. Every now and again, I feel like I can't breathe for missing my mom, but… it used to be every day, and now it's just… sometimes."

Afraid to break whatever spell had Sol sharing that much with me, I leaned against her, wrapping her with a single arm without looking away from the mountains that framed the sky in front of us.

"How long has it been?" I asked.

"Almost five years now."

"I'm so sorry, Sol. Do you want to talk about what happened?"

Sol shook her head.

"Not right now, no."

I nodded.

"If you ever… I'm always here. Any time. Day or night. You know that, right?"

Sol smiled, then turned and kissed my forehead.

"We'd better go help those boys. I think they might have gotten lost in the parking lot."

She turned and gestured to the wide lot full of rental cars behind us. It seemed like a sea of vehicles.

"Either that, or they decided not to rent to a bunch of teenagers, after all."

"It's possible. I told you we could use my——"

Sol was cut off by the roar of an engine, and a few moments later a black open-topped Jeep Wrangler, older than I was, came ripping into view with Trev behind the wheel and Seamus in wolf form hanging out the side gleefully, his giant pink tongue lolling out as he stuck his nose into the wind.

I laughed. Leave it to Trev....

"Your dream car awaits, Madam."

"Complete with loyal canine companion, I see."

I couldn't help but be cheered by the blatantly obvious attempt to make me feel better. How many times had I told Trev that when I grew up I was going to drive around in an old beat-up Wrangler, just like Dad, and take my wolfhound with me everywhere? I wasn't going to quibble if the wolfhound had been replaced by an actual wolf. Or a human that could turn into one...

<p style="text-align:center">~~~</p>

The house was exactly the way I remembered it. A small part of me wanted to kick the blue-painted, clapboard-clad, two-story bungalow for daring to be unchanged after everything that I'd been through. It had been both eerie and nostalgic, living there alone for the first few months after my parents had gone missing. Now, it just annoyed me that the house didn't show a single outward sign of the turmoil and confusion it had held within it for all those months. It remained nestled peacefully into the mountainside, surrounded by pine trees and a small bit of naturally inspired landscaping. Maybe kicking it would dislodge something, even a tiny fleck of paint, and transfer some small amount of the pain I'd lived through.

I took a deep breath, reminding myself that kicking the house wouldn't actually help anything.

Then I stepped forward and kicked the damned door anyway.

The door was unfazed. It remained the same dark red it had been a year ago, the color my mom had painted it, claiming it was lucky, the year that we had moved to the house. I had always suspected that she just found white to be completely boring, and I didn't disagree, so I had never asked.

And there were those damned tears again.

"Want to go a few more rounds with the house, Luv, or can we all go in now?"

That voice… was not supposed to be here right now.

I turned away from the house to find none other than Azrael, standing in all of their barely clad glory, wings tucked neatly against their back as they stood behind Trev, Sol, and Seamus, all of whom had turned to gawk at the scantily clad succubus.

"Hey there, Devourer of Souls," I said, trying not sound too damning. Gwen had made it sound like Azrael got a worse rap than they deserved.

"Oh dear. Someone snitched, did they?"

I nodded.

"Gwen ratted you out, but she didn't sound too condemning, really."

"Oh? Gwen *has* always been delightfully understanding, actually. So, she just told you the name, then? Left all the gory bits out?"

"There are gory bits?" I asked, trying to repress a shudder. I had thought that the name was likely metaphorical, or, if it were literal, that it at least didn't refer to something done physically.

"Well, racy might be a more appropriate adjective, really."

In a weirdly universal show of testosterone, I could feel all three of my companions perk up at this suggestion, and I couldn't help but laugh, especially since I found the idea intriguing myself.

"She didn't give us details of any kind, as usual. Just said enough to confuse everyone and then disappeared."

Azrael merely blinked at this statement, and when I didn't seem inclined to share anything else, said, "Well, are you going to fight the door again? If you're trying to kick it down, there are better ways."

I snorted.

"Well, I would use the keys, but they're lost in a pile of cinders at the moment." I sighed. "Still, I'm mostly just venting my frustration on the door. Why are you here? Dare I ask?"

Azrael sighed theatrically.

"Can't an angel visit their friends just to say hello?"

"Oh? Do you have friends here?" I asked, trying to sound cheerful. "Who are they? Maybe I know them."

"Is that any way to treat someone who saved your life?" Azrael replied. "I could have just let you die in that canyon."

"Seriously, Azrael, why are you here? I appreciated your help in hell and all, but you are not here for the warm fuzzies, so what gives?"

"Maybe I came for a snack?" they said, raising their eyebrows provocatively, and with entirely too much purr in their voice. I think I heard every single one of us gasp a little bit, and I wondered if everyone felt the same pulse of heat through their bodies that I did.

I shook my head, trying to refocus.

"Azrael, knock it off."

Azrael frowned, then sighed.

"You are trickier than the average wereleopard, aren't you?"

I shrugged.

"And if you wanted an easy snack, you would go somewhere full of regular humans, wouldn't you? Like a bar or something?"

Azrael smirked.

"I could… but it requires putting on clothes and *pretending*."

"You mean something aside from hiding the wings, I assume?"

"*And* you're smart… are you sure you don't want to give me a snack? You're entirely my type."

I smiled, trying to pretend that I wasn't tempted by the idea. I had to assume it was something to do with Azrael's magic that made me even consider the thought. I mean, don't get me wrong, their angelic forms were the most physically attractive people I'd ever seen, both the male and female aspects, but… some part of my brain couldn't stop picturing the tiny, red-skinned squirrel demon that had shrieked at me until I'd been willing to climb a three hundred foot cliff with no rope just to get away from it. Meanwhile, all my friends seemed entranced. Looking around, I realized I was the only one who had spoken since Azrael showed up, and the rest of them were all staring, slack-jawed, at the succubus.

"Can you, um… undo whatever has my friends unresponsive?" I asked.

"Oh, they're responsive enough," Azrael said, raising a hand to their own chest and running their fingers down the center. I was currently seeing Azrael's female form, as I assume everyone else was, since everyone here was attracted to females, and the move was… well, it made me rethink my squirrel demon prejudices.

I shook myself again, and looked around to see Seamus, Trev, and Sol all take a step closer to Azrael.

"Seriously, Azrael, that's enough," I said. "This seems eerily non-consensual."

That made Azrael stop touching themself and stand to attention.

"I *never* force people into anything. I never have to."

I quirked an eyebrow at that, as the moment Azrael stood up and stopped touching themself all three of my companions seemed to snap out of whatever had them basically drooling at the angelic figure before them.

"Ok, well, whatever you were doing was distracting them from what we came here to do." Since I didn't actually *know* what Azrael had been doing, I couldn't be sure it actually was non-consensual. "And besides, unless you clarify exactly how it is you feed, and what a person gives up, I don't think you can claim that it's consensual when someone wants to sleep with you. Wanting to have sex and wanting to give away a part of your soul are two different things, in my book. I may want one without the other. Savvy?"

Why I decided to channel a Disney pirate for that particular moment, I don't know, but it seemed to work on Azrael.

"Oh fine, I won't eat you or your friends. Happy?"

I nodded.

"I'm not sure I'm happy," Sol volunteered, raising her hand. "Depending on what's entailed, I might be willing to give up a small piece of my soul for some of… that." She gestured at all of Azrael's currently female form.

Azrael's face turned smug, and I couldn't help but laugh.

"Everyone is, of course, free to do as they please. I just don't want anyone becoming succubus food against their will."

Azrael raised one hand into the air, and placed the other on their breast in a way that was more than a little seductive.

"I vow that I will only take souls from you four when you volunteer," they said.

"Ok, can we finally get back to business here?" I was still unclear on why Azrael was here, but decided it wasn't worth wasting any more time finding out. Seamus and I may have been cleared by MOME, thanks to Albert, but Trev was still on MOME's most wanted list, and Sol was probably working her way up there, at this point. They could still be trying to track us down, and it was entirely possible that they had this house under surveillance. In fact, that was Trev's primary objective, for now. As far as we knew, MOME had no idea where this house was, but that didn't mean that they hadn't figured it out since then.

I turned back to the house. At least Azrael's appearance had thoroughly distracted me from the storm of emotions that looking at this place brought on.

"Trev?" I asked.

I didn't need to clarify. Because, twins.

"I don't detect any spells monitoring the place, but I can't be sure about video and sound without my—"

"Here," Sol said, handing Trev what looked like a small tablet.

"Thanks, but this doesn't have—"

"Yes it does, Avito. I stole it. It's yours."

"How did you—"

"Long story," Sol said.

I turned to look at her, wondering what the hell she'd been doing, going through Trev's stuff, but she just looked slightly embarrassed, shuffled her feet, and shook her head.

Ok. Weird. It appeared that something had gone down between those two while Seamus and I were locked up.

"There's a… no, got it. We're all good. As long as Sol hasn't tampered with this, we should be in the clear," Trev said, with a decided edge to his voice.

"I only took it because—"

"Ok, you two. I get it. There are trust issues. Apparently, we need to do a group session or something, but we might have limited time before MOME catches onto us, so can we please just… do this?"

They both nodded, and I turned back to the red door.

"Here goes nothing," I muttered.

I lifted my leg, and had just angled my body to get the leverage I needed to kick the lock when it exploded in a ball of flame in front of me.

"THE FUCK, TREV?"

"You'll just break your leg," he said. "The deadbolt is probably thrown, so kicking it won't work unless you're strong enough to kick out the whole frame. It's not a college dorm, Vic, it's a house."

I laughed. What else was I going to do? I had really been looking forward to inflicting some actual damage on the house, but Trev was probably right. Enhanced snow leopard strength aside, I was more likely to break myself than the door. Sometimes movies aren't the best guides for real life; true story.

We all plowed inside and I did my best to ignore the actual look of the house. Everything was exactly as I'd left it, from my parents' old coats hanging by the door to the forest green paint on the wall by the stairs. I didn't bother looking in the living areas. I headed straight for the stairs, then turned left to wrap around to the master bedroom. My parents' room.

I had tried packing their stuff up after they'd… when I'd known that they weren't coming back. I thought it would probably be healthy, or whatever, but… I just couldn't do it. Even the one time I went so far as to get a box ready, when I walked it to their room something had just felt wrong about it and I'd turned away at the door.

As I walked towards the door again, I got that same feeling, that something about what I was doing just wasn't right.

Weird, because I had no intention of packing up their stuff. Just one thing in particular, and something they'd sent me to go get, no less.

The closer I got to the door, the stronger the feeling got. I stopped in my tracks.

Just out of curiosity, I took a few steps back.

Sure enough, the feeling of wrongness lessened.

I took a few steps forward.

The feeling of wrongness returned, full force.

"Well, that's quirky," I mumbled, then jumped a foot in the air when Azrael suddenly appeared at my side.

"What is?" they asked.

"Damn it, Azrael, you scared the crap out of me!"

"Sorry, I wasn't trying to. I walk rather quietly."

I looked the towering angelic figure over, trying not to roll my eyes.

"And dare I ask why stealth is on the list of natural traits for a succubus?"

"Easy. Predator evasion," Azrael replied.

I raised an eyebrow at that.

"What predator can possibly be a match for you in this form?"

Azrael frowned.

"We are not the worst thing out there."

I shrugged.

"I never said you were, but it seems like you've got a handful of advantages in this realm that would make it difficult for anything else to make a snack of you."

I had used the term "snack" to be funny, but Azrael shuddered when I said it, and something about the way their skin paled made me wonder what could actually hurt this six-and-a-half-foot tall creature with a physique reminiscent of Greek statuary.

"I'm looking for something in there," I said, not wanting to get too specific, since I still had no idea what Azrael was really doing here. "Mind keeping an eye on the door for me?" I asked. "Just in case anyone from MOME decides to pop in."

Azrael nodded, and I walked to the door to my parents' room, despite the creepy feeling in my stomach forcefully telling me that it was a bad idea.

I WAS FAIRLY certain that the aforementioned creepy feeling was thanks to a spell, or whatever they called instances of magic in this world, my world—fuck, a lifetime of reading fantasy novels *should* have prepared me for this, but so far nothing matched up with my fictional expectations and I didn't even fully understand how magic worked here…. Whatever. I was going to go ahead and call whatever it was that was trying to repel me from my parents' bedroom a spell, because I didn't have a dictionary and no one was offering me free lessons on how this shit worked. Or if they were, we kept getting interrupted by people trying to kill us.

So this spell. It was making me want to turn right around and run in the other direction, but I was determined to get into my parents' room today.

Now that I had a guess as to what was making me feel like this, I was amazed that I'd never noticed it before, or rather, that I'd never suspected anything was weird about it. I had noticed it, I'd just thought that it was my gut response to packing up any of my parents' things, or even looking through them. But now… now I was going in with my parents' permission, or rather, at their request. So I shouldn't be feeling the wrenching guilt that made me want to turn around before I even got to the door.

"Hey, Azrael?" I asked, on a hunch. "Would you mind walking towards this door for me and telling me… if there's anything worth telling me?"

"That's incredibly vague, Vic."

"Yep. Trying not to skew the test results."

"Fine. You just want me to walk towards the door?"

"Yep."

"Alright."

So they did. All six-and-a-half feet of winged glory walked towards the door. And stopped about three feet in front of it.

"Odd," Azrael mumbled, then walked all the way to the door and touched it. "Very odd."

"Care to elaborate?" I asked.

Azrael stepped back from the door and returned to the post they'd been keeping at the top of the stairs.

"Mage spells rarely have any effect on me. My own magic in this realm is too strong for them to do much, but… I felt a twinge as I approached the door, and by the time I got to the door, I didn't particularly want to touch it. Which is why I made myself touch it, just to be sure it wasn't a compulsion taking effect. I was able to touch the door, so I guess not."

I nodded.

"That what you were expecting?" Azrael asked.

"More or less," I admitted.

And then I stepped forward, pushed past the feeling that was yelling at me not to go any closer, and turned the handle.

~~~

It was a bit anti-climactic to just find the room exactly as they'd left it. From the old kimonos they'd brought back from Japan with them, to my mom's aging katana, to my dad's old collection of Calvin and Hobbes books—none of it had moved an inch.
~~~

I don't know what I'd expected, exactly, but dust collecting on all of my parents' old stuff wasn't really it. And it wasn't even a creepy-haunted-house amount of dust. Just the regular no-one-has-lived-here-for-a-year-or-so's amount of dust.

What *was* strange was that some of that dust was out of place, now that I took a second look at it.

That is to say, there were some fingerprints in the dust over on the bookshelf by the closet. That was weird, but the fingerprints only marked an empty space on the bookshelf. So, all that told me was that someone had been here recently and stolen a book. That was possibly really terrible news, but I didn't know which book it was, and I doubted that it was my mom's mysterious hidden journals. I didn't think those were just going to be sitting out on a shelf. Besides, Mom had said "journals" plural, so there ought to be more than one slender volume missing between *The Hitch Hiker's Guide to the Galaxy* and *Good Omens*, if that had been what someone had taken.

Still, I decided it was probably worth investigating. So I squatted in front of the shelf with the missing book and took a good look at the empty space. Then, just to be extra sure of things, I reached my hand into the cavity left by the absent tome.

And hit my fingers against something that made a crunching noise, followed by a whirring, followed by a creepy creaking noise that totally would have fit with a much thicker layer of dust.

And then the whole book shelf popped off the wall and started to recede into the floor.

Because of course it did.

Because my parents had whole secret lives that they'd never told me about.

But apparently had written down.

On paper.

Lots and lots of paper.

Seriously, so much paper.

Like, holy shit, Mom, how many trees did you kill just to document your life?

The entire shelf *behind* the shelf that had just tucked itself away like a prairie dog on ball bearings was just as large as the first and it was filled with journals!

"Nice taste, Mom," I muttered, picking up one of the first volumes and noticing the nicely tooled leather cover.

I opened the cover and was quickly greeted by the date September 7th, 2000, in my mom's familiar handwriting.

I shut the damned thing as fast as I could, but my eyes were still soaked before I could even put it back on the shelf. Barely able to see, I gave up trying and just sat there and let myself have a bit of a cry.

"Vic?" Azrael's oddly British voice called from the doorway. "You alright, Luv?"

I wiped at my eyes so that I could actually see the angel lurking in the doorway.

"I think so. Just… probably haven't finished grieving my parents, you know."

"Ah… you lost them, did you?"

I sighed. Right. Azrael had no reason to know any of this yet.

"Yeah. It's kind of a long story. The super short version is, I'm an orphan as of like six months ago."

Azrael didn't say anything else, but suddenly was seated beside me and enveloping me in the most comforting hug I think I've ever experienced.

Which was weird, coming from a creature I'd only met a couple of days before, who had never presented themself as being entirely cuddly before. Maybe it was the wings that were joining in on the act. Wrapping me up in a warm cocoon. Whatever it was, Azrael had just moved to my "always accept hugs" list.

"Thanks," I muttered, still not letting go. "I wasn't expecting that."

"I'm not entirely heartless, Luv. Besides, I was really just being nosy."

I laughed at that.

"That may be true, but the hug helped. Is that succubus thing?"

"Nah. That's pure squirrel demon, that is."

I laughed again.

"I have a feeling I shouldn't ask…"

"Ask all you like, I'm not telling. A demon has to keep some secrets, after all. Anyway, I'm glad I could help a bit. If only for a moment."

I was about to reply, when I got a distinct whiff of smoke.

"Azrael? Do you sm—"

"Vic! GET OUT OF THERE! THERE'S A FIRE AND I CAN'T—"

Azrael and I were both on our feet before Trev could finish, but he was cut off anyway, and I had a terrified moment of panic before he sent a message to me mentally.

I'm fine, Vic. I was trying to fight the fire with my magic, but it's not working. Just like the stuff back at the boat. I was breathing deep to yell for you and took in too much smoke. Not sure why I didn't just start with this. Can you get out?

By then Azrael and I had reached the door and discovered that the landing was completely engulfed in flames.

Not by the stairs, I sent to Trev. *We'll try the window.*

We?

Azrael's with me.

And then I was too busy trying to open the nearest window in my parents' bedroom to worry about much else.

The damned locks wouldn't budge, and I had to suppose that a year's worth of weather and humidity fluctuation, without any upkeep, had taken its toll on the hardware. Luckily, after my wereleopard strength proved unequal to the task, Azrael ripped both locks straight out of the wall.

"Not subtle, but functional," I admitted.

"Come on, Luv. You first."

I almost complied, but then I remembered my mom's journals. The whole damned point of this mission, sitting on those shelves, and the flames that were now inside the doorway and not-so-slowly making their way towards the open window, which was now just feeding the fire with every gust of fresh oxygen that came through.

I sprinted to the hidden shelf.

"No time, Vic!" Azrael shouted from their spot by the window.

"I can't just leave them!" I shouted back, because we had to shout over the roar of shit burning like oil-soaked paper around us now. I grabbed the volume that I'd first opened and the one next to it, and tried to grab a few more and tuck them under my arms. Then I got to the window and cursed loudly. Then I coughed a bunch.

"You have to get out of here now, Vic. The smoke will get you soon, even if the fire doesn't."

And the fire was quickly approaching, even if the smoke was going to kill me first, and damn it all. I was going to break a leg if I made this jump in human form.

"I need to shift. Are those things decorative?" I asked, gesturing to Azrael's wings as best I could while trying to cover my nose and mouth with my shirt and shove journals into their arms.

Azrael just glared at me and took the books, all except one. That one I put on the windowsill just before calling on my snow leopard form, then picked it up in my mouth and leapt from the second story window into a small patch of scrub oaks.

I TURNED BACK just in time to hear a scream come from inside the house and then see Azrael disappear from the window.

"Did she just go leaping through a wall of fire?" Seamus asked, from behind me.

I nodded, but kept my eyes glued to the window. It wasn't worth shifting back to human just to correct Seamus' gendering of Azrael. After all, if he'd only ever seen their female aspect, why would he think differently? Besides, English is a bit stupid about gendering anyway.

It felt like a lifetime, but it was probably only about 90 seconds later when Azrael came flying out the window, carrying an unconscious Trevor, followed by a glorious full-panther-mode Soledad.

I let out an anxious roar, somewhat muffled by the journal still clenched between my teeth, and bounded over to them all, but Azrael just shooed me back.

"We have to get away from this house. I can't stop the fire either, and this place isn't going to be standing much longer."

I swallowed the anguished wail that wanted to rise out of my throat, and instead just turned and ran up the longish driveway to where the trees opened onto the main road. I could already tell that everyone was behind me before I shifted back to human.

"Trev! Trev!" I shouted, running to Azrael's side and putting my hands on my brother's throat, desperate to feel a pulse.

It was there, strong and constant.

"Just too much smoke," Azrael said. "I think he'll be alright."

"As you just reminded me, too much smoke can still kill you. He needs a doctor, or a healer, or whatever. Should we take him to the Tree of Life?"

Sol shifted to her human form.

"Too risky. MOME knows about the grove. He needs his girlfriend," she said.

I raised an eyebrow.

"Rhelia's healing gifts are well known," she said. "If she'd been able to treat you after that MOME spell hit you, there might not have been any scarring."

With Trev lying unconscious in Azrael's arms, I didn't waste time thinking about that, but instead focused on getting Trev to Rhelia.

"Group hug," I said loudly, trying to get everyone within my embrace.

Seamus and Sol both stepped in, and Trev didn't move.

"Probably best if I stay behind," Azrael said, handing Trev to Sol. "I'm resistant to most mage spells. I don't want to mess with whatever you use for transportation."

I nodded, unsure if Azrael was right about possibly messing with my magic, but unwilling to test it when it came down to getting Trev medical assistance.

With Trev in Sol's arms and my hands on both Trev and Sol, I took a deep breath, and instead of focusing on a place, I reached for the one person I desperately hoped could help my brother.

"UGH. OF COURSE I wouldn't get to keep an encyclopedia's worth of information about our parents lives. That would have been entirely too easy, not to mention too big an info dump," I muttered, flipping distractedly through the pages of the one journal that I had managed to hold onto from my parents' bedroom (thanks to Seamus, who had picked the damned thing up after I dropped it to run to Trev's side back in Colorado). Seamus had handed it to me right after we'd settled ourselves on the floor of Rhelia's Unterberg base of operations. Apparently, she had more than one place to call home in the world.

I was lying on a futon like the ones my parents had brought back from their time in Japan—the ones that are nothing like the thick mattress things you can buy at Ikea (did they even have Ikea in a place like Unterberg?) but more like deluxe sleeping pads, way better than anything you'd take camping, and great once you get used to them, but probably well below what most North Americans would consider comfortable. Sol, Seamus, and Trev were all lying on similar mattresses spread out on the floor around me, and the whole place made me think that Rhelia had probably read Shogun more than once. There were katana mounted on the wall, and the floor was covered in actual tatami mats. I was going to have to ask her about the decor once she finally got back from wherever she'd been rushing off to when we'd first arrived. She'd barely taken thirty seconds to assess Trevor and show us where we could put him, then she'd been running out the door.

"What?" Trev asked, from his futon on the floor.

"Nothing," I said, snapping back to the present. "Just that, since my life has apparently turned into some kind of adventure tale, it's no wonder I wouldn't be able hold onto all those journals that Mom wrote. I mean, hell, they probably answered every question I've had about Mom and Dad, since they disappeared and I found out that they were deep into a magic world I never knew existed."

"What do you mean, info dump? Vic, what the hell are you talking about? Your life is an adventure story?" Trev sounded mildly worried.

"You remember Gwen, yes?"

"Yeah…"

"Well, whatever kind of deity of good fortune she claims to be, when I first met her, she said she was my narrator."

"Your narrator?" That was Sol, apparently joining in the incredulity party. Not that I blamed her.

"Yeah." I snorted. "She showed up naked in the woods loudly describing everything I was doing."

"And you didn't run the other way?" Seamus asked.

I shrugged.

"She was ruining my weekend getaway, so I decided to talk her into leaving instead."

"Did it work?" Sol asked.

"Not really," I admitted. "She left eventually, but only after I insisted that I would take over my own narration."

"First person?" Sol asked. "Yuck."

"Why do people say that?" I asked. "What the fuck is wrong with first person narration? It's gripping and immediate."

"It's so… angsty," Sol accused.

"Yeah, well, you and the old goddess can go take a long walk off of the same short pier. I *like* first person narration. Besides, you would have said whatever was necessary to get rid of the creepy, seemingly insane woman who showed up and claimed to be your narrator, too."

Sol's eyebrows rose provocatively.

"Gwen? Naked? I doubt I would have been in a hurry to get away."

That had me laughing.

"Yeah, well, you were the first woman I ever found attractive, so… I wasn't as impressed."

"Well, I like first person narration too," Seamus said. "So, what's the deal? Why do you have a narrator?"

"I don't know, really. Gwen never explained. She just made it sound like 'they' were listening/or reading or whatever, and wouldn't know what was going on if there was no narrator. So I said I would do it, if it would stop her from standing around announcing every single thing I was doing and describing me like food."

"Ugh, I hate that," Seamus said. "I am not a fucking coffee with a touch of milk."

Sol laughed. "I actually enjoy being compared to chocolate, myself."

We all chuckled.

"You are, of course, welcome to describe yourself as all the delicious desserts you like," I said. "But I'm not about to describe you as one."

"Well, I think you're a mocha, anyway," Sol said, playfully running a hand along my arm.

I batted her away.

"It's not nearly as obnoxious when you do it, but *anyway*—"

"Yeah, I want to hear about why you're in a book," Trev interrupted.

"I don't know. And I'm not even sure it's a book. I mean, I honestly thought that Gwen was just nuts when she said all that, but… well, she actually does seem to be a goddess and stuff, so…"

"So, it's possible that you're in a book?" Sol asked, still sounding incredulous, but not quite as dismissive as she had a minute ago.

"I suppose? I mean, the day Gwen showed up was the day that everything started to turn completely weird."

"But if you're in a book, then that means we all are!" said Seamus excitedly. "At least, we are when we're with you."

I laughed again.

"I suppose so…"

"So, you're saying that all of those journals were burned to ash because it would be too easy for the plot if you found everything out from a set of books?" Trev asked, finally returning us to my original point.

"Well, I hope that's not the only reason. That would be lazy writing, and if I'm in a book I'd like to hope it's not one that's poorly written. But yeah, imagine reading a book that's full of fight scenes and chase scenes and stuff and then finding out most of the major plot twists because the character sat down to read something that spelled everything out."

"Ok. Blargh. Yeah, you make a good point," Sol admitted. "Still, if the book is written in the first person, it's entirely possible that's not very well writ—"

"Hey! Don't you start. First person narrative is a completely viable point of view and can be used to great effect. Fuck right off with your implication that it's a cop-out."

Sol raised both hands in a pacifying gesture.

"Please don't kill me, Gatita. I forgot that you read as much as I do, just in some different genres. Look, so if the writing isn't lazy, then we're still stuck with the fact that someone burned your old house down on purpose, most likely to stop you from reading those journals. We need to know who, and why."

"I may be able to help with that," said a voice from the doorway.

We all turned and looked at the same time, to find Rhelia standing on the threshold, holding what looked like a flash drive, along with my back-pack.

"**Y**OU KNOW WHO burned my house down?" I asked, before my brain fully caught up with what I'd just heard.

"Not exssssactly, no," Rhelia said, coming in and sitting down beside where Trev was lying. "But, between your file," she elaborated, handing me my backpack, "and what I have on thissss flash drive, we might be able to figure it out."

"Isn't the safe assumption at this point that it was MOME?" Seamus asked, as I began to pull my parents' file from my backpack.

I nodded.

"Sure, that's the easy bet. But if they knew about those journals, why leave that house standing for all that time?"

"Umm… to lure you in and try to kill you, for, like, the hundredth time in the past month or so?" Seamus stated, so matter-of-factly that I had to stare at him for a moment.

"Fair point. Well made," I admitted. "Still, it was a bit roundabout for MOME, don't you think? I mean, they haven't hesitated with the direct approach before."

"Yeah, but you just won your trial, and now if they just straight-up kill you, they will look really bad, even to their supporters."

Seamus was just full of good points tonight.

"I'm still fuzzy on why they care about their public appearance anyway. I mean, since when do dictatorships, or corrupt oligarchies, or whatever, care about public opinion?"

"Historically? Pretty much always," Trev replied. "It's how they keep uprisings down. They need to maintain at least a vague semblance of justice, or else the masses organize and then they're finally shit out of luck. And, if they don't look legit enough to keep the people they hire to dole out their 'justice' in line, then they lose all their power."

"What would Hitler have ever been able to accomplish without Nazis?" Sol added.

"Right. Ok. So, the MOME assholes have to at least *pretend* not to kill me openly. I admit, in that case, a house fire seems like a legit option. 'Oh how sad! The poor, recently exonerated Victoria Marmot was mourning the recent tragic loss of her parents, when a mysterious house fire took her life, and those of her troublesome and law-breaking friends.' Right. Makes sense. Still, I don't know that MOME knew about those journals. After all, if they did, why leave them there? They could have lured me there without the actual journals, just using the mere idea of them. And it still doesn't make sense that they could have found out about the journals anyway. Mom and Dad went to a lot of trouble to keep that from happening."

"Possssibly, but we cannot rule MOME out," Rhelia said, from Trev's side, where she appeared to be doing a Vulcan mind meld or some shit.

"What are you doing?" I asked, when her hand was still spread across Trev's temple and cheekbone few seconds later.

"I'm jusssst checking to make ssssure there isssssn't any tissssue damage in hissss lungsssss."

I was intensely curious about how that worked, but realized that with my luck, someone was likely to come tearing into the room with a flamethrower to destroy this file and Mom's last remaining journal any moment now. I should really start reading them if I had any hope of getting any answers, like, ever.

A half an hour later I knew a lot of things about my parents that I'd never known before, but I still didn't know who'd set my parents' house on fire.

"Trev, how far did you get in this file before you started that argument with Albert?" I asked.

Trev, no longer under Rhelia's ministrations that I could see, but now sitting up and holding her hand rather endearingly, tipped his head back as if to think.

"I got to the point where I found out exactly *what* they were studying with Albert."

"Ok. I read that part, but it didn't really make sense to me. Expanded Dark Matter studies? What does that mean?"

Trev took a deep breath and sighed.

"Its what they were teaching me and the other 'misfits' at MOME too. Well, some of us, anyway."

"But Mom and Dad went to learn it from Albert voluntarily?" I asked.

"Yes. Because when they were teenagers, the program actually *paid* them as test subjects, rather than merely kidnapping and then 'educating' them, but they were still more or less lab rats."

"How do you know that?" I asked.

Everyone else in the room seemed to be making a point of maintaining absolute silence, and I wondered what taboo we were getting into that had them all so quiet.

"Albert as much as told me that much, after I confronted him about it, but it was clear enough in the file itself. Besides, no one from our world who had anything left to lose would volunteer to be in a study on Expanded Dark Matter."

"Really? Why?"

"Because most people consider it a myth," Sol replied. "The most respected researchers in the magical world have disproved it's existence time and time again. There have been over a dozen articles published to that effect."

Rhelia snorted.

We all turned to look at her.

"Humanssss are sssso limited," she sighed. "Besssidessss, it hassss alwayssss been in MOME'ssss besssst interessssstssss that no one believe in Exsssspanded Dark Matter theory, sssso why would they let anyone 'prove' it, unlessss it wassss for their own purposssssessss?"

"So, did Mom and Dad even know what they were signing up for?" I wondered aloud. "Sounds like MOME wouldn't have made it public knowledge."

"Unlikely. Who knows how MOME advertised it back then, but they probably just said they were conducting a study and willing to pay qualifying participants."

"And how did one qualify?" I asked, a chill running down my spine.

"Likely by being on the list of 'dangerous persons' that MOME used to bandy about in those days," Trev replied.

"What does that mean?"

Trev and Rhelia exchanged a look that I couldn't decipher, then Trev stood up, muttered a word I couldn't quite make out, and a ball of light appeared, floating above his hand.

I just blinked at him, but Seamus and Sol both gasped.

Then he muttered something else, and the ball of light disappeared, replaced with a rock.

Sol and Seamus gasped again.

I just blinked some more. I mean come on, Trev could turn into a fucking bird made out of fire—why was this supposed to be impressive?

I must have said that last part aloud, because Sol replied, "Gatita, it's not that those are impressive tricks, it's just that they're mage tricks. A were shouldn't be able to do them at all."

I shrugged, feeling more out of place in the magical world than I had all month.

"Dark matter is dark matter, isn't it? Why wouldn't you be able to use it for whatever?"

Trev smiled, then banished the rock and bent over to hug me.

"That's the benefit of growing up outside the magical world, Vic. You aren't hampered by a lifetime of internalized propaganda. You are absolutely right. Dark matter is dark matter, and anyone who can access it, who has it running in their veins, should be able to pull on whatever aspect of it they like, even if they have a genetic predilection for certain ways of accessing it."

"Makes sense to me," I said, returning Trev's embrace.

"The dragonsssss have known thissss for millennia," Rhelia said, sounding a tiny bit smug. "We have tried to tell humanssss before, but you alwaysss wanted proof, and when we gave it to you, you ssssaid, 'but you are dragonssss, it issss not the ssssame.'"

Sol and Seamus both looked dumbstruck.

"It's even possible to access more than one animal form," Trev added, now seeming truly excited.

"Impossible," Sol whispered.

Trev and Rhelia exchanged another glance.

"You guys have been witnessing Vic pull us through time and space for weeks now, and you don't think that it's possible to have more powers than the ones that you're genetically predisposed towards?"

"But a goddess bestowed some powers on her," Seamus objected.

"And how would that work, if one couldn't access dark matter in different ways than the ones we're born to?"

"I don't know. She's a goddess?"

"Look, let's all go into the basement, and we can show you something."

"Well, that sounds ominous," I muttered.

Trev laughed, giving me a nooggie, and I wondered what was making him so giddy.

"We could go to the roof, but then the whole city might see, and that could be… complicated."

~~~

So, that's how we wound up in the creepy basement of a giant stone apartment complex in the middle of the night.

I was not reassured when Trev asked me to stand in the middle of said creepy, weeping-stoned room, and then asked me to close my eyes.
~~~

"Imagine yourself as a dragon," Trev said.

I laughed.

"What?"

Rhelia replied, "Feel the wind on your facsssse assss you fly through the ssssky. Feel the protection of the sssscalessss that cover your sssskin. Feel the raw power you contain within. Feel the ansssscient knowledge that you are an apexssss predator and none can sssstand in your way…"

I decided it would be faster than arguing to just keep my mouth and eyes shut and go along with the exercise, even if it was pointless. I didn't know what they thought was going to happen, but—

Everyone gasped.

"Yessss, very good!"

I suddenly felt… weightier… like I was taking up quite a bit more of the room, and… I could feel the stone beneath my… claws? with four feet instead of just two. What the fuck? Had I pulled on my snow leopard form without meaning to? But that didn't explain how much wider apart my feet felt, and, ah fuck it, I had better just open my eyes.

Um… am I a dragon? I asked Trev and Rhelia.

"Yep," Trev said proudly.

Looking around the room, I couldn't really argue the point.

I was a dragon.

S SOON AS I had opened it my eyes, it had been clear why we had done this here, rather than in Rhelia's apartment. When I looked down, everyone was way below me. My head was just shy of bumping the ceiling, and that was only because my dragon form seemed to have entered the world ducking. I couldn't quite see the end of my tail until I made a point of flicking it up off the ground and waving it at myself. I was coiled tightly, but if I had to guess, I was about the length of a soccer field. My scales appeared to be every color of a tropical sunset, from deep crimson to bright orange, and a thousand shades in between. The fact that I could even distinguish that many colors in this dank, candlelit cellar was strange enough as it was.

How am I a dragon? I asked. *It's not like I've spent a lifetime training how to access different paths in dark matter, or whatever you were suggesting it would take to do this.*

"You can do it because one of our ancestors was a dragon, so the pathway is there anyway, no practice needed."

"If it were that simple," objected Sol, "EVERYONE would have access to multiple animals, from birth."

"And to some degree they do," Trev said. "But two things keep them from accessing them. One is years of conditioning to make you believe that you can only access one form, and the other is lack of genetic diversity in were communities. How many non-panthers are in your family, Soledad?"

Sol stared at him for a moment, then nodded.

"Ok. Fine, maybe that's true, but we're not the only were community. You and Vic aren't the only weres in the world with parents of mixed heritage."

"That's true," Trev conceded. "But that brings me back to the first point. Conditioning. Have you ever *tried* to reach for a form other than your panther?"

Sol shook her head, then Trev turned to Seamus.

"Have you ever tried to reach for something other than your wolf?"

"Nope. I've always been pretty stoked about the prospect of turning into a wolf. Never occurred to me to try anything else."

"Right. Why bother?" Trev agreed.

"So are you saying that MOME actually taught you all of this?" Sol asked, slightly incredulous.

"Well, they didn't teach us the theory behind it, they only experimented on us by trying to get us to access different things. They wanted to see who could learn what, and how much dark matter access you had to have to be able to pull off certain things. All for 'research,' of course. I put together a lot of how it all worked on my own, but Rhelia is the one who brought it all together for me."

We all turned to Rhelia and she shrugged.

"Assss I ssssaid, dragonssss have known thissss for millennia. It wassss eassssy to share with ssssome-one who wassss willing to lissssten."

I suddenly found myself in human form again, apparently so I could voice the question, "What exactly were you doing in that dungeon again, any-way?"

I was a bit sad not to be standing there as a dragon anymore, but if all it took was remember-ing the physicality of dragondom, then I was sure it would always be easy. I was never going to forget what that was like.

"We should return to my apartment," she said. "It issss not ssssafe to disssscussss ssssuch thingssss here. Anyone could overhear ussss."

Unfortunately, before we could even question Rhelia's suggestion that this might not be a safe place to chat, a spell exploded over my head and the ceiling started to come down.

"TELL ME WHERE she is!!" cried the crazed voice of a vampire who I was really getting tired of seeing, as I felt the weight of a full-grown man plow into my back, hurling me to the ground.

"Gwendamnit, Edik! If your daughter wants to contact you, she will fucking find you. Now stop trying to get us killed!"

The room had already descended into chaos. I had no idea how many MOME agents were here, but I didn't stop to count. I pulled on my snow leopard form, clawing and twisting my way out of Edik's grasp as fast as I could, taking zero care not to injure him, and possibly throwing in an extra set of back claw scratches as I got myself out from under him.

Of course, you may be wondering why I didn't just flip myself back to my newly acquired dragon form, but there were many reasons for that. One, I wan't sure how to fight in my dragon form. Could I breathe fire? A cone of cold or acid? Ok, I might be leaning a little too hard on my D&D lore here, but I could have a breath weapon, or then again, I might not. And even if I did, I had no idea how to control it in tight spaces and not take out my friends. Plus, I filled up most of this room on my own as a dragon, and I did not want to crush any of the people I loved right now. Furthermore, my snow leopard was light and quick, and I was already very used to fighting with it.

I didn't hesitate to launch myself at the nearest MOME agent. After their attack on Seamus' moms, I no longer doubted that they had the worst possible intentions every time that they engaged with us, and I wasn't about to let them kill any of the people I cared about.

I had my work cut out for me, though. The room was crawling with MOME agents. Luckily, there were so many of them that they were reluctant to fling spells willy-nilly, and they'd brought more shifters than they usually did. This creepy-assed basement was starting to resemble the world's most fucked-up zoo.

A bear was launching itself again and again at Trev in his phoenix form, and Sol was facing off against an honest-to-Gwen Bengal tiger. Seamus was chasing after a giant-eagle-looking-thing that I didn't know the name of, but which was almost the same size as Trev's phoenix. Rhelia was calmly in her human form, deflecting the various attacks of what appeared to be a silverback gorilla, and there seemed to be mage upon mage filing into the room, setting off spells wherever they could get a clear shot that wasn't going to take out one of their comrades.

In short: shit had gotten real.

I heard screams and roars as intense heat flared behind me, and I turned to see Trev immolating not only the bear that had been attacking him, but also half a dozen mages who had been closing in.

Deciding that he seemed to have things the most in hand of anyone, I headed for Seamus and his giant-eagle-thing. Despite the fact that Seamus had the eagle on the run, he didn't seem to be faring too well. The mages all around them kept firing at him continuously, and when I looked more closely, it seemed like he was mainly trying to use the eagle for cover. Which was fairly clever, but not a great long-term strategy when your target has wings and you don't.

I decided to wait until the eagle was on the down-swing, trying to expose Seamus to mage fire and not looking in my direction, then I launched all furry two hundred pounds of myself at the giant thing, sinking my teeth into its neck. It collapsed quickly beneath my weight, making a sickening crunch as we hit the floor. I didn't wait to see if it would get up again, but instead put myself between Seamus and the mages that surrounded us. I was pretty sure that MOME would use the excuse of "apprehending" Trev and Rhelia as cover for killing Seamus and me, and it made me wonder why I had ever given credence to the idea that they might have been trying to find a subtler way to wipe me out.

Luckily, the mages decided that hitting their downed eagle friend was too risky for the moment, so Seamus and I had a second. I put my paw on him and shifted us both over to where Rhelia was deftly avoiding the attacks of the eight hundred pound gorilla. I figured that Rhelia was the most likely of all of us to be able to defend someone else at the same time as herself. She seemed to understand this, giving me a slight nod as I deposited Seamus by her side.

Then I leapt over to where Sol was facing off against a half-ton of feline might, the likes of which

I had only seen up close at zoos. Since I didn't know of any better options, I went with a standard flanking move, leaping for the tiger's hindquarters and sinking my teeth and claws into his haunches even as he slashed his giant paw at Sol's head once more.

My teeth and claws ripping into his flesh seemed to pull him up short. Indeed, he took a moment to turn and snarl in my direction, either to express his displeasure or simply to exclaim in pain. Either way, it was a mistake he couldn't afford to make, and Sol instantly pounced at the opportunity.

That is, she leapt forward and sank her own teeth into the tiger's throat.

Not that the move did an untoward amount of damage. The tiger was far from going down, even with Sol latched to its throat, but now it was thoroughly distracted by the close proximity of panther teeth to its jugular, and it was my turn to do some damage. So, I scrambled farther up the giant cat's back and spread my claws out into its shoulder blades, hoping to do a debilitating amount of damage.

I had a feeling that the gashes I was leaving in the otherwise pristine orange and black fur would turn my stomach, once I was back in human form, but my snow leopard had no qualms about fighting off a predator that was threatening my mate and family. For the moment, I was thankful for the desensitization, because I really didn't have time to agonize about whether this guy (and yes, I'd approached in a crouch from behind, so I had full confirmation that this tiger was a dude) had a partner, children, or any number of other innocent people attached to him who would be devastated by his injuries. The human part of my brain kept wanting to go there, but I was not in a human body, and my snow leopard didn't give a fuck.

The tiger seemed to give an equal number of fucks as he attempted over and over again to throw me from his back, all while trying to rip Sol's throat out. Luckily, she was tenacious and her jaw strength seemed unshakeable. She had added her front claws into the mix and was deeply anchored on the tiger's neck. I continued to rip and tear, hoping against hope that tigers were built similarly enough to bulls for my efforts to cause his head to drop. I'd only seen one bullfight in my life, and only on television, but that had been more than enough. The memory of the men on horseback spearing the poor thing's neck and shoulders, before the matador even took the field, had haunted me ever since.

If it came in useful now, though, it would be worth it. Worth it to protect Sol, to protect Seamus, to protect Trev…

I was starting to slide off the tiger's shoulders due to all the blood that was seeping from the dozens of cuts I'd spread across its shoulders and neck, and I lost my footing completely when the Bengal swerved wildly from the pattern he'd been following up to now. I rolled gracelessly to the floor, only landing upright thanks to the magic, possessed by all felines, that enables them to essentially defy physics anytime they need their paws under them.

Even with my paws under me, I slipped halfway across the floor, my paws grappling for purchase through the thick coating of blood that covered them. By the time I regained traction, Sol had disengaged from the tiger, who now lay thrashing feebly on the floor, and had charged the silverback that was attacking Rhelia. The choice made more sense when I noted that the gorilla had been joined by a… was that a moose? Crap. That thing was huge.

I was turning to join her when I heard a cry from behind me that sounded too much like Trev's phoenix for my liking.

When I got a good look at him, I saw that they had him in a huge net made of… something that looked like silver, but probably wasn't, because it wasn't melting and Trev burned *very* hot. Silver had a low enough melting point that it would have turned liquid the moment it got within a foot of him, if he was flaring, as he clearly was right now.

Before I'd even fully registered the cry, I had turned in his direction, and now I was racing towards him. I hadn't even covered half the distance between us, and he was surrounded by mages. Over a dozen of them formed a tight circle around him, half of them facing towards him, and half of them facing outwards. I was now dodging and weaving, hoping to avoid getting hit by another spell that would melt half of my skin off.

The barrage of spells that they sent my way was constant, and I soon found myself giving ground, backtracking slightly now and then, in hopes of dodging more of their attacks, but ultimately giving up more ground than I was gaining.

I let out a roar of frustration, then followed it instantly with a roar of agony as one spell hit my shoulder. I crumpled, but managed to keep my eye on Trev, who was slowly being maneuvered towards the same damp archway through which we'd entered. Without second-guessing the move, I pulled through time and space, shifting myself directly on top of him, hoping that I could shift both of us away from the circle of mages. Instead, I shrieked in agony as whatever that net was made out of seared itself into my skin. Trev cried into my mind, *No, Vic! Get away! This net is blocking everything I throw at it. They'll just capture you too. Please!*

The anguish in his voice, and the certainty that he was right, joined with the debilitating agony produced by that net to convince me to listen to him. I rolled myself to the floor, narrowly missing the grasp of a handful of nearby mages, then managed to shift myself away from the circle of mages, but still maintain line of sight to Trev.

So I was watching when Rhelia shifted into a dragon form that was far too large for this space and began destroying every MOME agent within sight. Her serpentine neck swayed, bobbed, and struck with such agility that the MOME agents closest to her never had a chance. I think she swallowed the silverback whole, and I was well beyond furious enough not to feel a moment's sympathy for the creature. They were taking my brother from me. Again. Fuck that!

I suddenly found myself on my feet. I was amazed, because the pain in my shoulder was intense, and I was fairly sure I was missing half of the muscle that was supposed to hold me up on that limb, but I shifted my weight to my other three feet and did my best to limp forward towards Trev.

Unfortunately, it quickly became clear why Rhelia hadn't shifted to her dragon form at the start of this fight. She was trapped by the room, and couldn't advance beyond the archway through which they were dragging Trev. Also, the space was far too small for her to use her fire on anyone, or she risked destroying the rest of us along with them. She was reduced to claws and teeth. Still quite formidable, as the men and women now lying in various segments across the floor had learned all too clearly, but not enough to catch the assholes who were dragging my brother down the narrow hallway. Though she did manage to grab a few of the ones that didn't move fast enough.

They threw spell after spell at her, but nothing stuck. Everything seemed to simply bounce off of her, or hit her and then instantly dissipate. Either she was ignoring the effects of the spells, or they did nothing to her dragon-scale hide. Watching her tempted me to shift to my own newfound dragon form and fight alongside her, but I knew that the two of us in here would crush every last soul that wasn't a dragon, and besides, then I would be just as stuck as she now was.

So, I rushed ahead in my snow leopard form, as fast as my injured right shoulder would allow, and launched myself towards the circle of mages that kept reforming around Trev. As if there were an unending stream of them, as if a new one popped into existence to take the place of each one that went down.

By the time I reached them, I could hear Rhelia bellowing in frustration behind me. Or, more accurately, I could feel it, as the sound shook my entire being, as well as the floors and ceilings all around us. I hoped that my charge forward hadn't gotten in the way of her attacks, but as far as I could tell, she was out of effective range already.

Before I could worry about it much, I was sinking my claws and teeth into the nearest mage and dragging her to the floor. She screamed, but she didn't fight me once she went down, so I leapt past her and towards my next target.

It was then that I felt a rush of fur, as Sol and Seamus both leapt at the mages to the left and right of me. The two of them tore into the mages with as much ferocity as Rhelia Marmot and I had, and I felt a renewed sense of hope as we plowed forward together into the circle of mages.

But that hope was short-lived, as they continued to pull along a thrashing, screaming, phoenix-

Trev, still wrapped in netting, and their numbers kept replenishing, no matter how many of them we took down. Sol and Seamus both seemed to have taken small hits and we were all nearing exhaustion.

Each swipe of my claws felt heavier and heavier, as if someone were gradually increasing the resistance on a weight machine that I didn't remember strapping to my wrists. Having to rear onto my hind legs repeatedly, just to swipe with only my left paw, made everything harder.

Seamus and Sol were faring marginally better, but Seamus, in particular, looked like he was nearing collapse anyway, and I wondered briefly if he was bleeding somewhere that I couldn't see.

Then an ebon streak of terror threw itself at the circle of mages.

Rhelia's battle cry was soul-shaking, and I half expected the cry itself to shatter the men and women surrounding her mate.

But it didn't. And neither did the series of attacks that she launched at them in her human form, though she did take down mage after mage, until she was practically in the circle of them, whirling in all directions, resembling nothing so much as a character from a modern kung-fu flick.

She even started flinging spells at them, something I'd never seen her do before, but which seemed to make no difference, considering how easily the line of mages replaced the fallen. They must have brought a hundred mages or more with them, keeping them all in the hallway while they sent in their initial force to distract us.

When none of that worked, Rhelia let out a final bellow and then threw herself on top of Trev. I assumed she thought that her weight would bear him down and then… I don't know, she would find some way to fight her way out with our help? Maybe that was her plan, but it didn't matter. The mages had wrapped Trev in as much spellwork as netting, and Rhelia's presence did nothing to dislodge him from their grasp. In fact, before I could do anything about it, they quickly threw an identical net around Rhelia, who screamed one more time before the whole mass of them turned the corner, disappearing from sight.

I put on a burst of speed, despite the protestations of my injured shoulder and aching muscles, almost collapsing when it came time to turn the corner, but they were gone.

"It's too late, Gatita," Sol shouted from behind me. "They'll have had a transport spell waiting, out of sight. They'll be back at MOME HQ by now."

I shifted back to human form, and nearly fell over as the pain in my shoulder flared. Right. I was going to have to remember that my snow leopard form had a much higher pain tolerance than my other half.

I slumped against the wall.

"Then get over here so I can shift us to MOME HQ."

"Not happening, Gatita. They would be waiting for us, and we'd be captured or killed in no time."

"Damn it, Sol! I can't just let MOME take my brother again!"

"I know. But we need a plan."

"Guys," Seamus said, finally joining us, in human form. "I don't feel so good."

I turned to look at him, and indeed, for someone who never wanted to be described as coffee with a touch of milk, he was looking awfully milky.

Shrugging off my own pain, I stood up, covering the distance between me and Seamus quickly. Just as I reached him, he started to slump. I caught him by the shoulders and could feel a slick wetness coat my fingers. Soon I was holding all of Seamus' weight, and my right hand was soaked in blood.

"Sol, he needs a healer. We just lost Rhelia, can we risk the Tree?"

"If I'd been planning this mission for MOME, I would have specifically left a unit there, in hopes that we'd be injured enough to need it."

"Damn it, what do we do?"

"It seems like a slow bleed. A regular healer might be able to help him. Take him to his parents?" Sol suggested.

Unable to think of anything else, I nodded, waited until Sol put her arm on my shoulder, and then shifted us to the small Unterberg apartment on the opposite side of town where Rhelia had arranged for Seamus' moms to stay.

I T WAS WITH no small amount of embarrassment that I learned that Rowan was a doctor. I really needed to work on asking my friends more personal questions. Especially the friends I was sleeping with, and might be fairly romantically attached to. I tried to give myself a break for it, since it had been a particularly trying couple of weeks, but it still bothered me that I didn't know the professions of my best friends' parents. At least I could console myself that I knew just as little about Sol's family…. On second thought, that didn't really make me feel any better.

Fortunately, since Rowan was a long practicing ER doc, I felt quite confident leaving Seamus in her care. Unfortunately, since Sol and I were likely to bring down a horde of MOME agents on any location where we were present, as far as I could tell, we decided it was safest to leave Seamus with his moms and try to find somewhere else to re-group, despite Rowan's protestations that she should really take a look at my shoulder before we went anywhere.

Of course, I couldn't really think of a place less likely to attract MOME attention than the place where Rhelia had hidden Seamus' parents, but, even still, we had a couple of errands to run before we could settle down anywhere anyway.

I shifted us directly to the middle of Rhelia's apartment, in hopes of avoiding whatever surveil-lance might have been left at her place. We didn't stay long at all. Just long enough to grab the jour-nal, the file, and—thanks to Sol, who spotted it on the floor just as I was about to shift us out of there—the flash drive that Rhelia had been carry-ing when she'd first come back to the apartment. It was ridiculous to think that had only been a few hours earlier.

I sighed as Sol grabbed my arm and I rallied to make another shift. I had a feeling this would be the last one I was going to be able to manage until I was able to rest, and/or get my shoulder healed. As such, I had one specific destination in mind, even if it was risky.

So it was that a certain creeptastic vampire managed to hitch one final ride back to Arizona with us. I didn't see or hear him, but I felt his creepily cold grasp on my shoulder as I was already reaching for the small, familiar glade that had saved my life so many times already.

While I was somewhat unsurprised to see Edik, as we landed in a tumble in the middle of the glade that held the Tree of Life, I was completely in shock when I stepped back and an ebon-skinned hand clamped down on his pasty neck, ripping it from his shoulders before I'd even had time to scream my rage at him.

I half expected to lift my eyes and see Rhelia, since she certainly had plenty of reasons to wish Edik dead, but aside from her being currently locked up by MOME, the skin of that hand was missing the iridescence that suffused Rhelia's skin. My brain had almost filled in the blank by the time I looked up to see Azrael, once more in her feminine form, grasping a very surprised looking Edik by the shoulder while his body slumped to the ground.

Then Azrael threw the head into the woods. My stomach turned at the sheer violence of the whole thing, but I couldn't get my brain to drum up any sympathy for the vampire.

"Umm… dare I ask what he did to you?"

Azrael shrugged. "I loathe vampires."

When neither Sol nor I said anything for a very long moment, they added, "It's a succubus thing."

"Right. Ok," I agreed eloquently, just before passing out.

WHEN I WOKE up, I felt infinitely better than I had in a long while.

"Dare I ask how long I was out?" I queried… possibly no one. I was staring at a beautifully tiled ceiling, but since I hadn't looked around at all yet, I had no idea if anyone was here with me. Something told me that I wasn't addressing an empty room, though.

It was Sol's voice that answered.

"Only a day, this time. Not bad, really, considering how many times you shifted us while missing a third of the muscles in your shoulder."

I sighed.

"Did Life heal me up? Or did we have to flee another herd of MOME agents?"

Sol laughed.

"No. No one was there besides Azrael and the Tree. Life healed you up, as usual, as soon as I took you over to him. Azrael ran off before I could ask any more about why they felt the need to decapitate the vamp, and then Gwen showed up out of nowhere and shifted us to Rhelia's apartment in the dragon realm, claiming that the dragons would be angry if you weren't turned over to their care."

"Huh. At least I didn't miss anything interesting."

Sol laughed again.

"I appreciate your sense of humor, Gatita. One of these days you're going to need a really good cry, though."

I chuckled, trying not to think about how right she was. I didn't feel like sobbing right now. I needed to—I knew that. I could feel it building up, threatening to tear my lungs apart if I let it, but… not yet. I needed to come up with a plan first. I needed to get Trev back. Get Rhelia back. Then I could sob for a while.

"I wonder why Gwen really dropped us here," I muttered, even as my eyes began to drift shut again.

"You think she has ulterior motives?" Sol asked.

"I think she's a goddess of good fortune who 'helps those who help themselves.' So she, at least, thinks that we have something to gain by being here. The question is, what."

"Indeed, that is an excellent question to ask, youngling."

That was decidedly not Sol, and I snapped my head towards the voice's origin just in time to see a woman who looked like she could have been Rhelia's sister walk into the room. Sol inclined her head respectfully as the woman came in, then left the room.

"Weird," I said, as the woman approached the bed on which I was lying. I now saw that it stood in the middle of a colorfully decorated room, tiled from floor to ceiling and draped with vibrant tapestries all over. "Sol isn't ever that subservient, in my experience. You must be Rhelia's grandmother, or some shit."

I liked the dragons quite a bit more than I liked the folks who ran Unterberg, but something about authority figures made me flippant, and this woman simply oozed "elder in charge of important shit," even though her human form looked no more than five or ten years older than Rhelia's.

"Ha! Rhelia said you were irreverent to a fault, little one. I like it. I'm not a fan of obedience, myself. And I can assure you that your friend didn't initially react to me with that amount of deference…. Though, I do hold a certain amount of respect for those who are old enough to have witnessed the beginning of the civilization from which I crawled."

She added that last bit with just a hint of reproach.

I laughed.

"It's not my fault that you're really fucking old, lady. I just got here. Do you have a name?" I asked, in a hurry to figure out who she actually was so I could be flippant without blatantly shoving my foot in my mouth every other sentence.

"You can call me Grandmere," she replied.

"Why would I use French to address you, and why would I call you Grandma, anyway? Are you actually Rhelia's grandmother?"

"More or less. And, as you are her ward, I am essentially your grandmother as well."

"First of all, weird. Second of all, I'd prefer to call you by a name. I already have a handful of grandparents."

After a long pause, I added, "Thank you for the offer, though. I appreciate how welcoming you've been."

She sighed.

"You can call me Siara. And, as to being welcoming… well, you are dragonkin in more ways than one, as you no doubt understand by now."

"Right, the whole turning-into-a-dragon thing… so that's really a genetic thing, and not some special power conferred to me by the whole my-brother-married-a-dragon thing?"

"Correct. I believe your maternal grandmother had a dragon form as well."

I thought about that for a moment, trying to remember if I'd ever seen Momo turn into a dragon, and when I couldn't come up with anything, decided to file it away under the giant-assed list of crap I was going to have to figure out later, after I rescued my brother and discovered what had happened to my parents.

"So, when you came in, you hinted that you might know something about what we stood to gain by being here."

"Did I?" she asked, with more than a hint of mischief in her eyes.

"Look, you don't seem like the type that allows for coincidental timing. We were discussing why Gwen brought us here and you waltz in, saying, 'that's an excellent question.' Don't pretend you don't have the answer. I'm not the type of person to underestimate you just because you come in a petite, feminine human package."

"Quite so," she admitted. "Well, Soledad has informed me that my granddaughter and her mate have both been taken captive by MOME. That is a crime we do not take lightly in the dragon realms. They have been warned before that they are not permitted to interfere with our people. Rhelia's previous capture was affront enough. We won't stand for it again, no matter what manufactured crimes they accuse her of."

As understanding began to take root, I sat up.

"What exactly are you saying?" I asked.

"We have reason to believe that MOME presents a threat, not only to dragon kind, but to everyone inhabiting the human realm you know as Earth, and all of its associated seams."

"So…"

"So, when you go after your brother and my granddaughter, you will do so with the full might of the dragon realms at your back."

S OL AND I spent the next day searching through every scrap of information we could piece together about what secret weapons MOME might be working on. It wasn't like we needed any more reason to go after MOME, as it was. We had more than enough. And with the dragons behind us, we might even have enough firepower to succeed. But that was the problem, *might* wasn't good enough for the dragons. It also wouldn't be good enough for the leaders of Unterberg, to whom Siara would shortly send an envoy, attempting to persuade them to join us. It would be difficult to persuade anyone to aid us, if we didn't have an accurate prediction of what we were up against. A possible army of misfit soldiers like Trev was one thing. A secret weapon that we were completely unaware of the nature of… that was something else entirely.

Thankfully, it didn't take too long before we found a few clues in the material that Rhelia had brought back to her apartment. My family file provided our first clue, buried in a note scribbled on the margin.

Both subjects present during incident 72197, but not directly involved. Subjects' exit interviews suggest they chose to leave program after incident due to rumors and in protest of research tactics used.

It was an oddly worded note, and I wasn't sure what it meant, but the fact that it was the only note in the margins of the entire file made me feel like it was worth looking into. Besides, we'd found precious little that stood out in their file up to that point. I mentioned it to Sol as something to keep an eye out for, which paid off a few hours later when she found another tidbit in the files that she was sifting through on the computer—the ones that were on the flash drive Rhelia had brought back.

Sol dragged me away from my mom's journal, which I'd just started on, after carefully going through the family file first, and plunked me down into a comfortable leather chair in front of a twenty-four-inch computer monitor. I hadn't realized that she and my brother had quite so much in common, until I saw her computer set up. From what I saw in this room, Rhelia was an accomplished hacker. Which probably explained where she'd gotten ahold of the files Sol had just been looking through.

Special investigation: Stripping Incident 7/21/97

After carefully considering patterns of destruction in the lab, the amount of damage overall, and the few notes retrieved from the site, we have determined that the explosion was a direct result of the stripping experiment. We recommend a full cease and desist for all experiments related to this research for the foreseeable future. The risk of another such incident is too great, and the results of the first experiment have clearly demonstrated the practice to be entirely inhumane.

That was a decidedly short and vague report, all things considered, but the thing that had me dropping my jaw and grabbing Sol's shoulder was the fact that it was signed, Albert Bumblebee & Evelynn Keeler.

Sol turned, caught my eye, gave me an emphatic nod, and I was gone.

~~~

Sol had probably wanted me to bring her along for the ride, but I wasn't sure that I had enough energy to take us both from the dragon realm to
~~~

wherever Albert was, and back again. Especially since I had zero idea where Albert was. My Gwen-given powers hadn't failed me, though. I had focused hard on Albert's presence and then, sure enough, wound up plopped into the seat of his red velvet wingback chair, complete with hissing, disgruntled iguana.

"Vic! What a delight to see you here. I don't suppose you've come with good news?" he asked.

I stared at his earnest face, partially covered by the thick white beard, bushy white eyebrows, and flowing long hair that made me wonder if he'd once looked up "wizard" on the internet and done his best to cosplay the whole thing. He was really nailing it. I still wondered if the whole thing was an act, though.

"Like what?" I asked. "Like, oh hey, found my parents killers, overthrew MOME, NBD? Just wanted to let you know? That sort of good news?"

"I'm afraid I'm not familiar with NBD."

"Don't worry about it," I said. "Not really what I'm here to talk about."

Albert only smiled beatifically and took a seat in the wingback across from me.

"Do tell," he said encouragingly.

"I'm here to ask you about the 'Stripping Incident.'"

Ah. There was the reaction I had been hoping for. Albert's face darkened, and his mouth turned down at the corners. I hadn't wanted to upset him, but based on even the vague description I'd read in his report, I could only assume the subject would be a bit of a downer. Still, I was relieved not to see blank indifference.

"What do you wish to know about it?"

"Everything you can tell me. I think it could be very important."

"It undoubtedly is, but I'm afraid I can't tell you about it if I don't know what you plan to do with the information."

I frowned. If that was true, then this was even bigger than I suspected. But if I told Albert the truth, would he still tell me what was going on? I didn't think he held any love for MOME anymore, but I didn't really know the guy. He could still be a MOME sympathizer, for all I knew. Still, I didn't think I could come up with an overly convincing lie, and besides, he might have some way to tell if I didn't tell the truth. If he was truly on my side, the truth would weigh heavily in my favor, and if he wasn't, then… well, I doubt I could trust anything he said anyway.

"I plan to use whatever you tell me to help take down MOME and get my brother and his mate back."

Albert smiled the smile of a hunter closing in on its prey, which wasn't completely reassuring until he said, "Right answer."

Then, of course, he took out a joint, lit it, took a long drag, offered it to me, shrugged dismissively when I turned it down, and then exhaled just before starting his story.

"I worked for MOME for many years, as I believe you now know. I worked in research for most of that time. That was how I met your parents. They both joined a study I was running in the mid-nineties. It wasn't long, however, after meeting your parents that I realized they were more than mere research subjects. They were both powerful enough to be at the cutting edge of dark matter theory, if they were willing to work with me. However, I already had reason then to be suspicious of some of my colleagues, so I didn't publicize their talents, nor did I change their status from that of research subjects, even though it would have been far more fair to call them colleagues. I didn't want them attracting attention from some of my less scrupulous workmates. We continued to work together to research expanded dark matter theory. Are you familiar with the concept?"

I nodded, not wanting to interrupt, but added, after Albert left an expectant pause, "Trev gave me a brief explanation and demonstration just before he was taken by MOME."

Albert looked dour again for a moment, but took another drag on his joint before continuing.

"Very well, if you're familiar with the basic concept then at least I won't need to prove it to you. So, your parents were already well versed in the concept of expanded dark matter and its possibilities by the time that the Stripping Incident occurred. Consequently, when they left the program immediately afterwards, MOME wished to keep an eye on them. That's only relevant later. First the incident itself. I can't be entirely certain *why* my colleagues were exploring it, but the evidence I found in the aftermath of the experiment left little doubt as to *what* they were experimenting with. They were attempting to strip a human who possessed dark matter in their blood of said dark matter."

Now it was my turn to frown.

"How does that work? And what would that do? Could you make someone non-magical? Why would you do that to someone? As punishment? That seems fucked up."

Albert only nodded, taking another drag on on his swiftly dwindling joint.

"All good questions, and indeed, it does seem fucked up. Unfortunately, I only have answers to some of your questions, and the rest is mere conjecture. I don't entirely know how they accomplished it, though I have a few guesses, and none of them are pleasant. Still, regardless of how they accomplished it, its effect was to destroy the entire laboratory and all of the people within it. It was only contained because of the way those laboratories are built. It wasn't the first time an experiment has ended in an explosion, after all. However, the destruction was thorough, and clearly unexpected, because all of the researchers for that experiment were in the laboratory, along with the recording equipment. If they'd thought that anything remotely like that could happen, they would have left all of the recording tools and at least some of the research team out of the room. So, we can assume they expected the potential effects to be contained within the test subject himself. Clearly, they were as wrong as it is possible to be, on that front. My suspicion, based on the resumes of the people involved in the study, is that, yes, they were attempting to find a way to make someone non-magical, quite likely as punishment, or simply as a weapon against MOME's many enemies. However, I have no proof of that. I do have proof that they were trying to strip the subject of his dark matter, although I destroyed that proof long ago, for fear that someone might decide to pursue the project's goal again. And, as I was put in charge of the investigation into what happened, I became more and more suspicious that the people who had ordered the experiment done were keen to take up the research project again. Eventually, they asked me if I would be willing to head up the group attempting to discern what happened, so that they could replicate the experiment. I declined, and that was when I retired from MOME. Your parents left immediately after the explosion. It was the final nail in MOME's coffin for them. They'd never particularly trusted MOME to begin with, but after all they'd seen while involved in my study, they decided to quit while they were ahead. They'd gained each other, and I vowed to destroy most of my notes on our research in hopes that MOME wouldn't take too great an interest in them. Unfortunately, everyone registered for my research was already marked by

MOME for a certain level of surveillance. Especially if they were likely to procreate."

My frown had been deepening throughout Albert's account, and now it reached a point where I was worried my mouth was going to break off my face.

"So that research is why Trev and I were MOME targets to begin with?" I asked, putting everything together as quickly as my brain could keep up. "Because my parents had been red flagged somewhere, so as soon as MOME put it together that they'd had kids, MOME came after us?"

"I'm sad to say that, yes, that is likely the entire reason that MOME attempted to kidnap you, and successfully kidnapped Trevor, all those years ago."

I felt a lot of emotions run through me at that news, not least of which was rage, but I reminded myself that this was all a ten-year-old hurt, and that I had more pressing things to focus on.

"But why do they want him now? They sacrificed dozens of agents to get him last night. I mean, I get that they want him back because he might know too much, but… that's a bit extreme."

"I cannot say, for certain."

"That sounds like an evasion."

"It is."

"Why?"

"Because I fear the answer might drive you to extremes."

"What can you tell me about MOME's secret weapon?" I asked, hoping the quick change of subject might elicit an honest response.

"What weapon is that?"

"I'm not sure. That's the problem. My parents left a… message, suggesting that MOME had been working on a secret weapon, but that they didn't know what it was. They also suggested MOME might be creating an army of people like Trev."

Albert pulled on his joint until the flame reached his fingertips, then winced as he extinguished what was left in a large ceramic ashtray on the small table next to his chair.

"Well, I can confirm that they've trained up a few hundred people like your brother over the past few decades, but I doubt any of them can match your brother in raw power."

"What? What do you mean?"

"Your brother, and you as well, come to that, possess the most raw access to dark matter of any human I've ever encountered."

"How can you tell?" I asked, a small warning bell starting to go off in the back of my mind.

"I've developed a spell that can detect dark matter in others. I cast it on most everyone I meet."

"Would MOME be able to tell the same thing?" I asked, more warning bells joining the first.

"They have their own methods, though I haven't shared this particular spell with them. They've likely run every test imaginable on Trevor, though. Over the years that they had him in custody."

"Albert… how powerful was the man they stripped of dark matter in that experiment?" I asked, despite being terrified that I already knew the answer.

"Not very powerful. He barely qualified as magical at all. I imagine that's why they started with him. They assumed it would be easy to strip him of what little power he had. And it's a good thing, too. If he blew apart the room with barely any dark matter within him, imagine what someone with any real power might do. Why do you—"

I didn't have to interrupt Albert. He cut himself off mid-sentence. Then he leapt to his feet.

"Oh bugger."

"Yes. Bugger about covers it."

"Vic, we have to get your brother back immediately."

"No shit, Sherlock."

"Wait—did you say they'd taken his mate, as well? Who is his mate?"

"Rhelia. How did you not—"

"Oh fuck. Vic, take me to the dragon realm immediately. Please."

Since that was where I was headed anyway, I didn't hesitate.

I SHIFTED US back to the room where I'd left Sol, ostensibly Rhelia's office, but Sol was gone and the lights were all off. Only the cool, dusty scent of a unheated home in fall greeted us.

Albert cursed.

"Where is Siara?" he said.

"I have no idea. I've only met her once, and she came to me. I don't even know where everyone else lives, in relation to where we are right now. I haven't had much time to explore."

"Right. Then follow me."

He had conjured a largish ball of light and was halfway to the entrance of Rhelia's home when the doorway flooded with light, outlining the petite shape of Siara before us.

"Albert, always a pleasure."

"Siara, I hate to be rude, but we have urgent matters to discuss. I believe we know what MOME's secret weapon is."

Siara stepped through the doorway into Rhelia's home, waving a hand, which somehow set all the lights ablaze.

"What is it?" she asked.

"My brother," I replied.

~~~

"Explain," Siara said, as Sol pushed her way into the house through a crowd of what must have been weredragons. They were peering curiously through the door, making me wonder what exactly Siara had been on her way to do before we'd shown up with news about MOME's weapon.

"They plan to turn Trevor, and possibly Rhelia, into a dark matter bomb."

"There is no such thing as a dark matter bomb," Siara said decisively.

"There is now," Albert replied. "I'm afraid all of our worst fears about Rebecca have come to pass, Siara."

"Wait, Rebecca?" I turned to Albert, my eyebrow raised in disbelief. "Rebecca Dryer?" I suppose it could have been some other Rebecca, but
~~~

how many Rebeccas worked in the higher echelon's of MOME?

"Indeed," Albert said, turning away from Siara to confirm my suspicion. "She is the head of MOME's Department of Justice, and she has finally taken full leave of her senses. I have questioned her morals for nearly a century, but this is too far by half. She is risking the stability of the entire world. Or worse."

"Wait. What?"

Don't get me wrong, I was already prepared to put everything on the line to stop anyone from turning my brother into a weapon of mass destruction, but the entire world being at risk? I hadn't made that leap yet.

"Beyond the devastation that you would personally experience, and of course the annihilation of whatever location Rebecca decides to target, my own research has led me to believe that these kinds of explosions might cause irreversible damage to time and space, the effects of which might be worse than that of a black hole."

"Wait, you've been studying these kinds of explosions? Does that mean you've created *more* of them?"

"Heavens, no, Vic. That would require killing innocent magical beings, which I would never do on purpose. No, I've spent the years after I retired from MOME searching out natural occurrences of similar phenomena. Mostly through a telescope. That's why I relocated to Flagstaff. Excellent skies there, not to mention the observatory. Easy to track interstellar phenomena."

"I'm afraid we don't have time for an astronomy lesson, Albert," Siara interrupted. "We have to get Trevor and Rhelia out of MOME's grasp before it's entirely too late. The question now is, where do they intend to strike?"

"Who benefits if they blow something up?" Sol asked, speaking for the first time since she'd entered the house, albeit after she'd given me a quick hug and a gentle punch in the arm for leaving her behind.

"Rebecca's goal has always been to gather as much power as she can get her hands on," Albert said, with a sigh. "In that, at least, she has always been consistent. At least, since her parents died. Before that, she seemed hell bent on doing whatever would please them most, but after… it's as though they left a hole that she could only fill with power."

"That's weird," I blurted out, before I could stop myself. "I mean, hey, don't get me wrong, everyone grieves in their own way, but… 'I'm grieving and the only thing that will make me feel better is oppressing everyone around me'… seems like a slightly wacky way to do it."

Albert shrugged.

"I'm not even convinced that it's grief. It may just be what she chose to do with her newfound freedom. We don't have time to analyze her motives, I'm afraid. We simply need to predict where she will strike."

"Well, if she wants power… who does she most need to take it from?" I asked.

"She's already largely in charge of MOME. There's no branch more powerful that the Department of Justice, and she has all the other leaders there in her pocket, either through bribes or blackmail. So, she doesn't need much help controlling the magical world on Earth."

"So Unterberg, then? Or here?" I asked, wondering how in the hells she planned to mount an attack through a seam. Although she had just attacked us in Unterberg two days ago, and we still hadn't figured out how, exactly, other than the fact that Edik had led all the MOME agents there somehow.

"Her biggest threat is muggles," Sol said. "Non-magical people," she clarified when Albert and Siara simply gave her blank looks. "They have guns, tanks, biological weapons, and nukes. Magical power can do a lot against those, but the magical world never had their own nuclear equivalent until now. If she wants to be in charge of ALL of Earth, then she needs to get the muggles in line. Which, in her mind, she can only do by showing them that she has something stronger than a nuclear bomb."

"Would stripping Trev of his dark matter really cause an explosion *worse* than a nuke?" I asked, chilled to my core at the very thought of it.

It was Albert who answered.

"Undoubtedly. Although Rhelia would cause an even more devastating swath of destruction, so it's difficult to tell which one they would use first."

I felt like sitting down, all of a sudden, but I put a hand on Sol's shoulder to steady myself instead.

"Trev," I whispered. "He would be the demo. Worse than a nuclear blast, but still not as bad as what they could do if people don't comply. Save the big guns for long-term threat."

I wanted to vomit, even as the words passed my lips.

"Where would they set him off?"

Sol jumped almost a foot in the air, then put her hand in her back pocket.

"Oh fuck," she said, as she lifted up her phone and the blood left her face.

"What is it?" I asked.

"Apparently they're planning to set him off in La Paz," Sol said.

"What? Why La Paz? How do you even know that?"

Then she handed me the phone.

"From my abuelita," she added, her voice barely more than a whisper.

Her screen showed a picture of Trev, tied to a statue in the middle of a circular plaza I'd never seen before. He was surrounded by a bunch of marble buildings and some nice landscaping, but his face was one of pure pain, and he was still tightly bound in that damned metal net that they'd captured him with.

"Perhaps they chose La Paz because—" Albert began.

"I wish I knew what that shit was," I muttered, passing the phone to Albert and Siara, who were already hovering anxiously over my shoulder.

"What shit is that?" Albert asked, looking closely at the photo and seemingly forgetting whatever he'd been about to say before I cut him off.

"That weird metal netting they used to capture him. It repels magic, or something. It was excruciating to touch, and it wouldn't let me shift us when I tried to grab him."

That had Albert zooming in on the photo, and I was surprised to see how easily he dealt with the tiny supercomputer he held in his hands. I didn't usually expect folks with white hair to have a firm grasp of cell phones.

"That, my dear, is Technetium—assuming they found a way to stabilize it—a metal not naturally found on earth. And I would bet dollars to doughnuts that is precisely what they are going to use to strip him."

"WHAT?" everyone else in the room asked at once.

"Non-magical scientists believe that it breaks down too quickly to remain anywhere in the universe, other than in the stars in which it forms, and that is why it does not exist outside of said stars, though copious amounts of it are created on Earth as a part of the nuclear fission process. However, I have a different theory as to why it does not occur here naturally. I believe that it reacts with dark matter in a rather... dramatic fashion. I believe that is why it is never found outside of the stars in which it is created. I believe that as soon as it is ejected from the stars that create it, it reacts with the dark matter available, creating the dark energy that is pushing our universe apart. When this happens in the vacuum of space, it is largely unnoticeable, certainly by most human forms of detection. When it happens around other matter, however.... It's the only thing that might possibly, if put in direct contact with the dark matter inside an individual, be able to accomplish what Rebecca wishes to do to your brother. They would need to inject it to cause that kind of reaction however, and in the meantime, she appears to be torturing him with it externally in the form of that net."

"**W**ELL, FUCK," I summarized, for the room. No one had moved from where we stood, in the center of Rhelia's beautifully decorated living room, a setting that now seemed a strangely cheerful counterpoint to the rather horrific topic at hand. We were surrounded by comfortable looking couches that no one seemed inclined to make use of, and colorful tiles with bright patterns and warm lines.

"Yep," agreed Sol.

"Indeed," added Siara.

"We need to break Trev free, like, yesterday," I said.

"Could you?" Albert asked.

Everyone returned their shocked expressions to Albert's serious visage. This time, I really wasn't sure what he was talking about, though.

"Could I what?"

"Could you break Trevor free yesterday?"

"You mean, like time-travel?" I asked.

"Precisely."

"You got a time turner hidden in your sweater?" I asked, nodding to the grey cable-knit he was wearing, baggy enough to look more like a bath-robe than anything. "Looks like you could hold a whole horde of treasures in there."

Part of my brain was shouting at me that we didn't have time for stupid jokes, but part of me insisted that none of this was real. That the entire thing had to be some kind of stupid joke, so why not throw some humor around?

"I do not know what a time-turner is, though the name is rather descriptive, but I would say that *you*, my dear Victoria, are the time turner to which you refer."

"Gwen gave me powers that let me reach through time and space to move around, but I've never—"

"Never tried moving only through time? If the power takes you through one, it can take you through the other. They are merely coordinates on a map."

Weird. Despite the fact of always thinking about how Gwen's power let me reach through time and space, I'd really never considered the time aspect. I mean, I may have had my world turned upside down in the past few weeks, learning that were-wolves, leopards, dragons, and every other damned mythical/fantastical creature existed, but… time travel? Surely that was a bridge too far.

"But, if time travel were possible, surely everyone would be doing it? I mean, wouldn't someone like Rebecca Dryer be using it to go back and put herself in charge of every major government in the world? In the realms? No one would ever die, because everyone would be going back and saving them/curing them, discovering the secret to living forever, and then going back and administering it to everyone they loved? I mean, come on."

"Certainly that might be the case, if everyone could do it, or if more than a tiny group of people could do it. But I'm not sure you realize quite the gift that Gwen has given you. She has only demonstrated how to use the power by traveling from place to place, and by the way, to my knowledge, you are the only non-deity who can travel between the realms without using a seam. Something I didn't realize until you brought me directly to see Siara. I had expected you to take us to the nearest seam, then teleport us to her from there. You—"

"Albert! Seriously. My brother is tied to a fucking post in the middle of a square, waiting to be blown up, along with an entire city!"

"My point is, Vic, that if you can jump through points in space, you can do the same with time. It shouldn't even take much more effort, just some flexibility of mind."

"Surely there are a ton of risks inherent to that? Couldn't I destroy the space-time continuum, or something?"

"The space-time continuum is, by nature, self regulating. Hence the 'continuum.' It is an oft worried about piece of fiction, but in reality there should be no possible way to ruin it. If you change the past, the future automatically alters itself, and if you create a paradox you must inherently ruin that timeline, but it will likely snap to the nearest available alternate timeline, or create a new one."

"Ok. THAT. Right there. Sounds terrifying."

Albert shrugged.

"It's all theoretical, of course, but my point is that while you can likely ruin things for yourself, in your own timeline, I doubt very much that you have the power to destroy the whole universe entirely, even if you destroy the universe in a single timeline."

"How does that even make sense? Doesn't the universe include all available timelines? I—" I stopped talking, shaking my head to force away the cascade of thoughts that wouldn't let me get to the important part. "Look. I don't think I can do that. I'm pretty sure I wouldn't be able to figure out what to do in time to save anyone, so can we go with plan B, or whatever? I need to save my brother."

P LAN B, IT turned out, was to just go in with
guns blazing. Siara sent someone else to appeal to Unterberg for help. Meanwhile, she
brought a hundred dragon shifters with her to the
street in front of Rhelia's home which we'd chosen
as our base of operations. The hundred she
brought with her would go in the first wave, and
she'd left instructions for reinforcements to follow
behind us should they be needed.

We had to hope that MOME didn't know that I
could shift that many of us from one realm to the
next without going through a seam first. Honestly,
we had to hope for a lot of things. If this went
wrong, we were about to get a whole lot of people
killed, ourselves included.

~~~
~~~

In order to maximize our element of surprise, we decided I would shift us all into a spot in mid-air and everyone would shift into dragon form upon arrival. The main reason for the plan was that my brain couldn't handle the idea of shifting a hundred dragons through time and space as easily as it could fathom shifting a hundred people. Apparently, everyone from the dragon realm who had signed up for this mission had no qualms with being dropped into the air a few hundred feet above La Plaza Murillo.

The sky was a cerulean blue and there was not a cloud in it. The air was crisp and fresh, despite being in the middle of a city of half a million people. I barely had time to notice any of that, though, or even take note of where Trev was, before I was free-falling through the sky and trying to call on my dragon form.

Thankfully, it responded quickly to my call and then I enjoyed a crash course in flying. I snapped my wings out, and they caught the wind with a deafening crack that shot me upwards at a terrifying speed. Panicking, I tried to drop my wings, but found them buffeting in and out awkwardly as I tried to lower them slowly, so I snapped them shut instead. Of course, that caused me to plummet towards the ground again. Terrified of hitting the ground, I spread my wings wide again, and this time, apparently clear of whatever updraft had grabbed me before, I began to glide in a gentle arc towards the ground instead. By the time I circled back around to where everyone else was, I was rather enamored of flying and vowed to practice it more often, assuming I survived everything that was about to happen.

Or… everything that was already happening, I corrected, as I looked at the scene unfolding in front of me.

The dragons were mowing into the MOME forces that lined the plaza, and the only thing that seemed to keep them in check was the fact that there appeared to be some non-magical people wandering nearby, as if they'd been curious to see what all the fuss was about. As a result, the dragons were mostly using teeth and claws to destroy the MOME agents that surrounded the plaza, the majority of spells flung their way simply ricocheting off of them, and the attacks of the few shifters present hardly grazing their hides.

It was easy to see why MOME had considered the dragons a big enough threat to try to eradicate them, even though the mere thought of doing so was completely despicable. One had to appreciate just how much damage the dragons could do when provoked. Of course, one also had to take into account just how far one had to go in order to provoke the dragons to begin with. They had spent centuries in peace with everyone else in the known realms. It had taken the abduction of two of their own and threat to the entire world, before they'd been willing to bring this down on MOME.

I looked around to see if I could spot Sol in the fray. She had come in on the back of one of the weredragons who was better at flying than I was (which is to say, ANY of the other weredragons), since I hadn't been confident that I wouldn't send us both crashing to our deaths. I barely caught a glimpse of a tiny (relatively speaking) black figure darting in and out of the mass of dragons and mages clashing on the ground before I refocused on my primary objective.

In the quick plan that we had hashed out before embarking on this whole endeavor, I had been given a very clear assignment: do whatever I could to free Trev before Rebecca Dryer, or whoever else she'd put in charge of the task (of course whoever applied the syringe would likely be killed in the blast unless they were able to make an incredibly fast escape, so there was little to no chance that it would be Rebecca), could inject Trev with liquid

Technetium. Or, barring that, kill whoever was going to inject him.

He was exactly where he'd been in the photo sent by Sol's abuelita, tied to a somewhat phallic statue in the middle of a small, nicely landscaped circle in the middle of the plaza. He'd clearly been tied there in order to draw the maximum amount of attention from the camera crews that now crowded around that center circle. Indeed, we'd realized during our planning that the only reason Rebecca hadn't set Trev off immediately, before we'd even known what they were planning to do, is that she intended to gain maximum visibility before doing so. After all, her threat would be that much more effective if she had the eyes of all the world leadership on her for her demonstration. And only a live feed would work, because any and all equipment close enough to get footage would be entirely destroyed by the blast. If she wanted any long-lasting record of the event, she would need to have coverage from afar. I wondered if she had cameras placed miles and miles from here, to try to capture a video of the explosion from a distance.

Of course, even if she did, they wouldn't be all that helpful if she managed to take out the entire earth with her. She had grossly underestimated the effectiveness of her own weapon, or was willfully ignorant of the additional risks—either way, she had to be stopped, regardless of the cost.

I still wasn't caught up on all the physics behind how it worked, but essentially the introduction of unstable Technetium into blood that contained large amounts of dark matter could easily cause a wave of dark energy strong enough to destabilize any nearby seams, thus potentially sucking our realm into another realm, and possibly destroying both of those realms in the process. And that was *on top* of my brother and half a million innocent civilians being killed. Not to mention all the dragons that I'd just shifted in here to help kick MOME's ass.

So, when I saw a person in a white hazmat suit approach my brother, with one arm outstretched, I didn't hesitate. I dove as fast as the wind would allow me, wings tucked tight to my sides and nothing between me and my target but thin air. I really hoped that I wouldn't take Trev out in my attack, but he would be dead either way, if I didn't get to this asshat before he got to Trev, so it was a risk I would just have to take.

I crashed into the earth hard, even though I flared my wings a bit just at the last second, and plowed through the grass and stone of the circle surrounding the statue that Trev was tied to. Before I let myself even register the pain of the stone impacting my scales, or the features of the person underneath the hazmat suit, I shoved my head forward, pushing past the line of stone that had finally stopped my slide forward, and snapped my jaws around the person whose arm was still outstretched to Trev.

"NOOOOOO!" Trev screamed, his face contorting with more pain than I'd ever seen on a human face. "RHELIA!!!"

For a moment I thought he'd somehow mistaken me for Rhelia, even though our dragon forms looked nothing alike. Even though there was no way my brother would ever have made that mistake.

And then my brain caught up with the truth, and I opened my jaws to allow the person in the hazmat suit to fall to the ground. The small window in the face of the suit showed an unmistakable visage. Ebon skin, ebon hair, and yellow, unblinking eyes.

"NO," I WHISPERED, amazed to find myself in human form again, my arms wrapped around Rhelia's waist, though I couldn't remember moving. "No! NO! It can't be her! Why is it her? WHY? She would never have agreed to inject you. She wouldn't! It can't be her. It can't be—"

Rhelia, why? A whisper in the distance.

I looked down and saw the syringe on the ground, which she'd most assuredly been about to inject into Trevor, but it still didn't make any kind of sense. Why would she have volunteered? Why would they have let her? She would just have died with Trevor, while causing an even larger catastrophe. Did she not know that? Had they told her something else? Did she think that her dragon's scales would save her from the explosion? Or did she just want to die with her mate?

My brain couldn't land on any explanation that made sense, and I couldn't fathom how a single bite from my dragon's teeth had been enough to end her. That didn't make sense. Rhelia was invincible. She was death on wings. She couldn't be killed, least of all by me. She could kill me a thousand times before I would ever get close to her, I was sure of it.

"Trev? What happened? Why is it her?"

But Trev was sobbing uncontrollably, and wouldn't answer. I was sure it was that he wouldn't, and not that he couldn't, because he could have spoken to me through our twin bond, but all I felt through that bond was despair. The worst kind of pain that a human could experience, as though I'd torn a part of his soul away from him.

"What do I do, Trev? What do I do? How do I make this right?" Tears were streaming down my face and my voice was barely audible around the grief that choked me, but I didn't know what to do. My brother was going to die because of a thing I had done, and I didn't know how to make it right.

Could you?

Could I what?

Could you break Trevor free yesterday?

The memory surfaced like a bubble in a pond, clear, and shiny and destroyed with the mere swipe of a hand… but it was there. And before I could think of anything else, before I could say anything, before I could even take another breath, I was reaching through time and space, but in this case, mostly through time.

I HAD MOVED entirely on instinct, or what I thought was instinct, using some tiny backwater of my brain that understood better than I did what was going on. Or maybe it was just that the thing I wished to see most in the world right then was a living, breathing Rhelia. One who hadn't just had the life crushed out of her by my dragon jaws. One who wouldn't stare blankly at me as I screamed her name over and over again.

"Rhelia!" I gasped, mostly in surprise, as I found myself staring into her eyes once more. Her living, seeing eyes.

Before she could even acknowledge my presence, I threw my arms around her and held tight, hoping desperately that she wouldn't find the personal contact an invasion of her space.

"Living Cat, are you well?" she whispered, returning the embrace, much to my surprise and relief. "You sssseem disssstressssed."

Yeah. You could say that. Or well, someone could. I couldn't, because I was too busy sobbing into Rhelia's hair.

When I could finally breathe clearly again, I said, "'Well' is not the word that I would choose to describe myself at the moment, TBH."

"TBH?" she asked.

"Oh, come on. I know you spend as much time on the computer as Trev does, you must know that acronym."

She laughed, then.

"Sssssomeone hassss been ssssnooping while I've been locked away," she responded, then stepped back a bit and took a good look at me. "Why are you here? You cannot hope to ressssscue me from thissss placsssse, ssssurely?"

I took a deep breath, noticed said breath was full of dank, moldy smell, and finally took a look around.

"What, does *every* MOME headquarters have its own dungeon?"

"Mosssst of them were built long enough ago that they do, but in thissss casssse, we are in what wassss left of the Bolivian HQ. Ssssomething about not wanting to rissssk anymore officessss, in casssse our friendssss wanted to come get ussss? The guardssss were a bit all over the placsssse with their thoughtssss. They sssseemed nervoussss."

Indeed, we were standing in the middle of a dank stone cell, surrounded by solid rock walls and thick metal bars. At least they'd left enough light in here for Rhelia to see by. It was a nicer accommodation than my last MOME visit. I reached out to touch one of the metal bars and instantly recoiled. It burned the way that the netting surrounding Trevor had.

"Technetium," I muttered, as I checked my hand for damage. "I'm amazed I was able to shift myself here."

Rhelia nodded.

"Indeed, I did not exsssspect to ssssee you. Where did you come from?"

Ah yes, that was a legitimate question, but how to answer it? And what good would that answer do? Could I shift Rhelia and myself out of here? And even if I could, would that save Trev? What would happen in the future if someone else were holding the needle? Would I kill them in time? Would they inject Trev sooner? How could I be sure I wasn't going to make this whole thing worse?

There was no way to predict what would happen if I changed things, unless…

"Unlessss what, Living Cat?" Rhelia asked.

I ignored the reminder that my thoughts tended to be an open book for Rhelia and the other dragons, focusing on the thought that had just tickled the back of my mind.

"Unless the person holding the syringe in the future knows exactly what's supposed to happen and plays along," I said, realization dawning on me. "Albert was right, time does fix itself."

Rhelia gave me the kind of smile that would have terrified me if I'd thought I were her prey. Luckily, we both had bigger game in mind.

I T DIDN'T TAKE Rhelia and me very long to come up with a plan, especially after I asked her a few pointed questions about how they were being held. Perhaps unsurprisingly, they were each being used as collateral against the other. If one attempted escape, the other would be killed, and vice versa. It wasn't particularly creative, but it was effective. Of course, once I informed Rhelia of MOME's true intentions (which, thankfully, she had suspected already—thus cutting my explanation time in half), she was more than willing to take the necessary risks. I just hoped I was right about how this was all supposed to play out.

The reason I was able to shift in and out of Rhelia's cell, it turned out, was that the cell was not lined completely with Technetium, so I was able to shift through the rock bed instead of the areas where the bars covered things. Meanwhile, for Rhelia and Trevor, who were unable to shift through time and space as I was, the prison was quite effective. They didn't have time to dig through the rock bed before a guard would come running, and the Technetium kept them from even touching their bars, let alone somehow manipulating them out of the way.

I probably *could* have shifted Rhelia out of there with me, but I discovered not long after I settled into her cell that I was truly exhausted from everything I'd already done that day. Not only had I shifted myself to the past, and straight to Rhelia's prison, I had also shifted an army of a hundred weredragons straight from the dragon realm into the human realm, then changed into a dragon, taught myself to fly right quick, and attacked and killed one of my new friends. It had been a rough day, by any stretch of the imagination.

So, I wasn't going to shift Rhelia anywhere before I got some rest. Instead, Rhelia and I talked for a long time, switching to our mental-only channel for all of the important bits. To an outside observer, it probably looked like two really tired people just staring at the walls and each other for a long time. Then it probably looked like I fell asleep for a few hours.

Probably because I did.

I woke to a quick slap across my face.

"You musssst go. They are coming."

I nodded and, without another word, I shifted, hoping against hope that the next time I saw Rhelia she would be alive and well, not a blank-eyed rag doll hanging limply in my arms.

~~~

When I arrived in front of Siara, she damned near dropped the ceramic bowl she'd been drinking soup from.

"I do not appreciate being surprised, youngling," she said.

I smiled, though I doubt the gesture reached my eyes.

"Then you're not going to like anything I have to say."

I looked around the room we were in, a modern kitchen by all appearances, complete with tile backsplash and a fancy kitchen island with a butcher block counter, and I wondered if she had brought all of this back from an Ikea in the human realm and installed it herself, or if she had somehow transported a fully finished home from the human realm to here, or somehow managed to get
~~~

human contractors to come work on the place in the dragon realm. The last seemed particularly unlikely.

"When you have finished admiring my home decor, would you mind telling me why on Earth you are here? You are supposed to be discerning what weapon of MOME's devising your parents were attempting to warn us about."

At that reminder, I took a moment to look at the clock. Then I sat down at the nice, lightly stained pine table that held Siara's bowl of soup.

"Hmm… right. I suppose that makes sense," I muttered.

It was only an hour before I would be back with Albert, and Siara clearly wasn't in the middle of rallying her troops, even though she should be, at least according to how things had played out in my earlier timeline. (Earlier? Ugh, talking about time once you'd started messing with it was hard. The last first time I did this? Maybe. Maybe that.)

When that vague statement and my wildly shifting thoughts simply earned me a cold stare from Siara, I tapped my fingers against the table for a moment, then added, "Siara, how quickly can you assemble a unit of 100 or so weredragons who are good at changing form mid-air?"

~~~

It was the next hour, watching myself (which was fucking trippy, by the way), Sol, Siara, and all the weredragons assembled outside of Rhelia's home, that was the most trying. I had tucked myself into the darkened doorframe of a house across the path from Rhelia's, as there was almost nothing I could do at this juncture. There was no point in shifting myself back to "the present" (an arbitrary distinction really, but one that I had to cling to for the moment, because I lacked a better term), when that would just exhaust me and I knew that I would need the energy soon. And the only thing that showing myself now would do is confuse the hell out of the me that was already here, along with all of the other people that me was already talking to. And I didn't think it would do any good anyway, although a strong part of me wanted to take the me that was already here and tell her in advance what was about to happen. Just to spare her some of it… but I shook that thought away, and huddled close in the stucco archway of the tastefully designed home that sat quietly in the night across from Rhelia's. One thing was for certain; if everything went as planned, I really needed to spend some time exploring the dragon realm. It was a truly lovely
~~~

space, and I was extremely curious as to how and where they managed to design and build their homes.

~~~

In the final minutes before we were all about to group together and launch our attack, I saw a strange shadow on the house next door to Rhelia's. Unable to discern what was causing it, I began to edge closer, but when I was halfway across the path, I ran into Siara.

"You should ride with me," she said, pulling on my arm.

I gave her a puzzled look. The me that was already here was supposed to fly on her own because she needed to learn to fly without risking anyone else's life, and so she would have the freedom to strike hard and fast against whoever was going to inject Trev. Siara knew this, she'd given me the damned assignment.

"I'm supposed to be on my own. I need to—"

"I'm certain the other you has that covered," she replied, before I could finish.

My mouth was doing a solid impression of an oxygen-starved fish when she gently took me by the arm and led me away.
~~~

"I can drop you where you need to be," she said, as we joined the ranks of weredragons circling up to be shifted by my earlier self.

I nodded dumbly, following after her, and didn't bother to ask how she'd figured out that I was a future me, deciding that the less we discussed it the better, most likely. By the time earlier-me was ready to shift us all to La Paz, I'd forgotten entirely about the odd shadow.

S IARA LANDED QUICKLY and cleanly in a shadowed corner of La Plaza Murillo, de- positing me without comment and taking off again almost in a single graceful movement. It made quite the contrast to the sunset-colored hot mess of a dragon who was currently banking wildly in the sky, trying desperately to learn how to fly in a brief handful of seconds—which is to say, me. Earlier-me, I guess. Though we were both getting pretty close to being present me, and I wondered what the hell was going to happen then? Would there be two of us forever, now? Did one of us have to die? Were there going to be infinite mes throughout the universe now? Were there already infinite mes throughout the universe? How the fuck did this shit work? Time travel was complicated.

It was also freaky as hell.

Here I was, crouched in the shadow of a large shrub, out of sight of most everyone, watching myself in dragon form—which, can I just say that I make a beautiful fucking dragon? I looked like somebody's Pinterest board for the coolest possible dye jobs, but instead of just my hair my entire body was covered in gorgeous, shimmering scales that ranged from deep crimson to bright yellows and blues, and every shade of purple in between. Anyways, here I was, watching my dragon form careen wildly through the sky, knowing what it had felt like to go through every moment I was watching, but feeling like it was a distant memory, because so much had happened in between. I think I had only gone back a single day, but it felt like a century had passed since I'd held Rhelia, limp and lifeless, in my arms.

And now my stomach was churning as I watched myself dive steeply towards the ground, aimed straight for the person in the white hazmat suit. I'd been too busy watching my former self's seemingly drunken flight pattern to even notice her appear at first, but she was there, and reaching out for Trev, even as my dragon form speared through the sky right for her.

Watching me hit the ground, and her, at such high velocity almost made me throw up, and I was weirdly grateful that I hadn't eaten much in the dragon realm.

"NOOOOOO!" Trev screamed. "RHELIA!!!"

And then I was running forward, without making a conscious decision to do so, my legs pumping me out of the bushes and towards the spot where a hurt and confused earlier-dragon-me stared incredulously at a limp figure in a hazmat suit. And, suddenly, I was filled with the worst kind of dread. Had Rhelia lied to me? Had she volunteered for this because it was the only way we could figure out to keep Trev from dying?

A cold knot formed in my stomach, heavier than any lead ball, as I sprinted the last few steps between me and Rhelia. Then she was in my arms, and I was leaning over her, sobbing, and dragon-me was gone, and there was no other me here, which means I must have caught up to myself, but Rhelia still wasn't moving.

"No," I whispered, once more staring into her too-blank eyes, dread coiling through my entire body.

No! NO! It can't be her! Why is it her? WHY? She would never have agreed to inject you. She wouldn't! It can't be her. It can't be—

"Rhelia, why?"

She wouldn't have done this. We had a plan. The plan made sense. She wouldn't have lied to me. Why would she have lied to me?

Trev? What happened? Why is it her?

Could I go back and fix it again? How many re-dos did I get? What would it take to fix this?

"What do I do, Trev? What do I do? How do I make this right?"

How could I be here again? How could I be holding onto this limp, bleeding—

No, wait. I took better stock of my hands—they were dry. She was wearing a hazmat suit, but still… dragon teeth are huge. Could it all have been pooling inside?

I took a better look at the body of the woman I was holding. There were tears in the suit. There should have been holes throughout her entire body, but there was no blood. No blood anywhere.

Rhelia? I sent the tiniest whisper.

*Convincsssse them, Living Cat, they musssst **believe.***

I sobbed. I let all the tears come. I could tell, somehow, that Rhelia had directed that thought only to me. She must have done something to cut herself off from Trevor…. Shit. Poor Trev. But for some reason Rhelia wanted everyone, even Trev, to think that she was dead, and she had sounded desperate. I didn't know what her plan was, but the least I could do after all of this was help her out. So I let the tears come. All of them.

A year of grieving over parents who had turned out to be people I didn't really know. Ten years of mourning a twin everyone else pretended was never there, and letting them make me forget. Shooting a man who was holding a gun to the temple of an innocent person. Being held captive by people who wanted me dead. Having a fucking lowlife vampire show up in my bedroom uninvited and having to fight him off. Watching that same vampire get decapitated by a vengeful succubus. Losing the only homes I'd ever known. Losing everything I owned. Seeing a woman I admired, respected, and liked die at my own hands, or at least believing that's what had happened. It hadn't been a great year, really, and I let it all come out. I mourned it all. Right there, in front of a hundred television cameras that had been brought to witness some devastating event, I cried like my soul had been torn out. I cried harder than I'd ever cried in my life.

And then had to pull myself together, because shit was about to hit multiple fans, and I couldn't even keep track of them all. MOME agents were rushing towards us. Probably coming to inject Trev anyway, but they were going to have to race Trev, who was straining against his bonds, reaching for the damned syringe which had somehow managed to land barely a foot away from him.

Trev, no! It won't just kill you, it will kill everyone in this city!

But Trev either wasn't listening or didn't care, and he was straining like a madman against the netting that held him in place. Damn it if he wasn't inching his way closer and closer to that fucking space metal that was likely to kill us all and take the whole damned world down with it. I tried to scrabble sideways, with Rhelia still in my lap, but she was a lot heavier than a five-foot-nothing petite woman looked, and I wasn't going to get there before Trev, damn it, unless I dumped Rhelia on the ground. if I did that, MOME might get to her before I did, and then we were just as screwed as if Trev got the syringe, because Rhelia would make an even bigger bang than Trev, and Gwendamnit, I needed some help!

Which was right when Sol pounced onto the backs of the two closest MOME agents and I decided I had enough time to drop Rhelia and launch myself at Trev, who already had his fucking fingertips on the syringe—and how did he even get down here, when he was supposed to be tied to the fucking statue? Did I knock him loose when I crash landed?

But I didn't have time to figure out how he'd loosened his bonds enough to slide down to the ground, or to worry about anything at all, except diving at Trev to make sure that he didn't jab anyone with that damned syringe.

And now we were fighting for the syringe like the Gwendamned climax in a freaking Bond flick.

TREVOR, DON'T DO THIS. I PROMISE EVERYTHING WILL BE OK, TREV. PLEASE, YOU HAVE TO BELIEVE ME.

I really hoped that no one else could hear me mentally shouting at Trev, but damn it, I had no other choice. He might have been restrained by that fucking Technetium netting, but he was thrashing like a madman. Probably in hopes of just accidentally spearing himself with the syringe, which, to be fair, there was a fairly high chance of at the moment.

Finally, I clamped my fingers around the syringe and pried it from his hand. For a brief moment, I was grateful that he was weakened from being trapped in that netting for days.

Then I took a good look and realized I wasn't really all that grateful. His face was as pale as Albert's, and he looked like he'd lost about twenty pounds. If I didn't know any better, I would have guessed he'd been doing multiple rounds of chemo for the past six months.

"Take him and go, I've got the rest of these douchewhips."

Sol was standing over Rhelia and assessing the next squad of MOME agents that were quickly approaching.

"You can't take them all on your own," I said. "Besides, I don't know how to get him out of this netting, and I can't shift him anywhere with it on."

"Perhaps I can be of assistance with that," said a British voice I hadn't really been expecting to hear anytime soon.

"Albert?" I asked, looking up to find the grey-bearded man stooping over Trev's other side. "Does this mean that you've already dealt with Rebecca?"

"I'm afraid not," he replied, while doing something I couldn't see to Trev's bonds. "May I have that syringe, my dear?"

I hesitated. I won't lie, I didn't really trust this thing in anyone's hands but my own. How could I be sure he wouldn't just turn around and use it for something else? But then I heard MOME charging us in the background, Sol's snarl as she resumed her panther form, and the battle cries of a few dragons as they dove to engage the enemy.

I handed Albert the syringe.

"If I am correct," he said, taking the syringe and carefully removing the plunger so that the liquid within could be poured out, "pouring this liquid form of Technetium onto these bonds will make them at least partially malleable."

"And if you're wrong?"

Albert's eyebrow arched, even as he remained focused on the task his hands were attending to.

"Then we might all die horribly, but what else is new, eh?"

I laughed. What can I say? My tolerance for dark humor had grown substantially over the past year.

"Ah there we are," he said gently. And, before I could really tell what he was doing, he had somehow unwound the netting that surrounded Trev's whole left side and then begun to pull him out.

I jumped up to help, grabbing him from the right, and in less than a minute we had Trev clear of the remains of the netting.

"Take them both, Vic. Take them both and go. We will deal with what remains of MOME here."

This time I didn't hesitate. I grabbed Trev by one arm, bent us both down to grab Rhelia with the other, and pulled us all to the safest place I knew, my heart breaking slightly at the knowledge that I was leaving Sol here to fight alone.

No, not alone. Backed by a hundred weredragons.

I saw her leap at a mage and tear into his shoulder, just as La Plaza de Murillo faded to blackness.

THE GLADE WAS quiet when we arrived, and I must have put us right in front of that scythe-holding oak tree that I had come to know as Life, because I could feel myself healing the moment I arrived. Indeed, I could see the color returning to Trev's skin even as I reached past him to start getting Rhelia out of that damned hazmat suit.

"What are you doing, Vic? Leave her be. Can't you just leave her in peace? Haven't you done enough?"

Each of those words cut me like a physical blow that the Tree of Life could never heal, but I didn't let them stop me.

"No, Trev. Not nearly enough, yet."

The hazmat suit tore surprisingly easily. It made me wonder if it had really served the purpose it advertised. Of course, it would make sense that MOME wouldn't have been too worried about actually protecting whoever they sent to inject Trev with that shit, as no amount of hazmat gear would stop that person from being atomized along with everything else in the vicinity, or worse. Still, it was weirdly harrowing to see how thin the suit was, and it crumbled as if it were cheap plastic that had been left in the sun too long.

YOU CAME JUST IN TIME.

I jumped, and sat up from where I'd been peeling at Rhelia's suit to see that Life had decided to take his ambulatory shape and come for a visit.

"Did you need us?" I asked.

NO. IT IS THE OTHER WAY AROUND. YOU NEED ME. AND YOU HAVE CUT IT VERY CLOSE, AS THE HUMANS SAY.

"What do you me—" I started to ask, just as Trev collapsed beside me.

I AM DOING ALL I CAN FOR HIM, BUT IT WILL BE DIFFICULT. THE RADIATION HAS BEEN ATTACKING HIM FOR DAYS, IT WOULD SEEM.

"Radiation? But I thought the syringe was—"

IT WOULD HELP IF HE WERE NOT FIGHTING ME.

"Fighting you? He's trying to keep you from healing him? Fuck. Trev!!!" I collapsed beside him and held his hands. "Trev, please. Don't go. She's not gone. She's not, I swear. Please, you have to listen to me!"

But Trev's eyes were closed, and his face, while pained, seemed absent. Like he wasn't quite there. Not knowing what else to do, I turned to Rhelia.

"Rhelia, now would be a great time to come back. We're going to lose Trev. He thinks you're dead."

YOU MEAN THAT ONE IS NOT DEAD?

I looked panicked between Life, standing over my brother, and Rhelia, lying prone on the ground.

Rhelia! You have to come back now. Trev is dying and he thinks you're gone, so he's not trying to save himself!

I am ssstuck, Living Cat. I did not craft thissss enchantment. I assssked her to leave a channel in placsssse sssso I could sssspeak with you. You will have to convincsssse Trev that I am sssstill here. Or elsssse remove thissss blasssssted sssspell.

If you didn't put it in place, who did? Who managed to visit you in there who was interested in helping?

Your Gwenhwyvar. She wassss very eager to be of asssssssstancsssse.

"Gwen! Gwen, we need you!"

SHE HAS BEEN RATHER BUSY TODAY. WHAT IS GOING ON IN THE WORLD, THAT SO MANY PEOPLE NEED GOOD FORTUNE AT ONCE?

I could think of a few things that would qualify, really. Of course, of course she was off helping with a battle to save half a million lives and overthrow a tyrant, rather than here with my entire world crashing down on me. That only made sense.

It still pissed me off, though. I knew Trev wasn't going to believe anything I said now. I'd heard the pain and contempt in his voice when he'd accused me of "doing enough" to Rhelia. He blamed me for her death, not unreasonably, and he wasn't about to listen to anything I said about her being alright until he could sense her living presence on the other side of their bond.

I realized, perhaps belatedly, that he and Rhelia shared a bond similar to the one that he and I shared. It was different, in that it wasn't a bond forged since conception and reinforced through eighteen years of life, but it was a bond of love, and a mate bond, and being mated as a dragon, whatever that meant. It was strong, and Trev thought it was broken. Until he felt it in place again, there was nothing I could say that would convince him Rhelia wasn't dead. And until he believed that, he was going to let radiation poisoning eat away his life.

So I did the only thing I could think of. I grabbed Rhelia's hand, and I followed our own bond. The one that she'd left open, so that she could contact me—the only person who was supposed to know that she wasn't really dead. I was her ward, and apparently that meant something too, because I could feel a place for her inside me, a place that I had thought was shattered when my teeth had sunk into her flesh less than an hour ago.

I followed that bond with… I'm not sure what. My essence? My magic? Some part of me that was transferable. Something that was me, but that I could manipulate and move outside of myself. Was that dark matter? Whatever it was, I moved it. I sent it flickering along the bond that held us, and I pushed it further, searching for Trev within Rhelia. I wasn't sure that made any kind of sense, and I sure as shit didn't know what I was doing, but that felt right. There must be some part of Trev inside of Rhelia, the same way that there was a part of him within me. It was what formed the bond, I figured. Tendrils of one person anchored inside of another, and then they were always connected, even when they were apart.

I could sense the parts that were Trev now. The ones inside of Rhelia. They weren't quite the same as the ones within me, but they were unmistakably Trev. Fiery. Fierce. Loving. Kind. Goofy. Fun. They held all of that, and more. Stubborn and reckless, too. It was all there. But they were blocked. There was something between me, between Rhelia, and that part of Trev. Not knowing what else to do, I pushed some of the bits of Trev that were within me against the ones inside Rhelia. At first I thought nothing was happening, but then, slowly, the parts within Rhelia started to writhe, as though they could sense their own kind and wished to reconnect. So I pushed them further, and also added a bit of the Rhelia that I had been surprised to find within me as well, and now the parts of Trev that were within Rhelia were jumping like a live wire.

I had a brief sense of misgiving as I pushed further, worried what it would mean that I was crossing these lines. These bonds that were so personal might never be the same, after what I was doing, and I didn't know how to undo anything that I did, but Trev was going to die. I couldn't let that happen. I couldn't. I'd lost too damned much lately to lose him again too, and… damn it, even if I hadn't, he was my twin. He might never forgive me for what had happened with Rhelia, but if he never lived long enough to hate me and love her, and do whatever he was going to do with his life, then I would never forgive myself, for any of it.

So I pushed again, mixing my own Trevor-bond with Rhelia's and my Rhelia-bond with Trev's Rhelia-bond, and this was fucking weird to put into words, but the words didn't matter. What mattered was that after a few more moments of this strange mingling, I felt a flash of energy, like touching an electric fence, and then I heard Trev cry out.

When I opened my eyes, still holding Rhelia's hand, and now holding Trev's as well, though I wasn't sure when I'd grabbed it, I saw Trev's face, streaked with tears, a faint smile curling the corners of his mouth.

He can ssssensssse me.

THE BOY HAS STOPPED FIGHTING ME. AT LAST HE BEGINS TO HEAL.

So, now tears were streaming down my face, too.

Rhelia's face was still the mask of death, including the blank, staring eyes that had chilled me so the first time that I'd seen them, but I now understood that all of that was simply part of the enchantment that Gwen had placed on her.

"What a touching scene," said a voice I had been certain I would never hear again.

"**F**UCK, EDIK, YOU'VE really let yourself go," I said, standing up and putting myself between my brother and the vampire, who was really channeling his inner Walking Dead right now. His head looked like it had only loosely reattached itself to his neck, and his body was coated in mud, dead leaves, and what looked like a few forms of fecal matter from various woodland creatures. His face was in only marginally better shape, and looked like an owl had crapped on it.

"It took me a rather long time for my body to find my head, but thanks to the healing properties of this glade, I was able to survive."

I gave Life a rather judgmental glare, but the tree merely shrugged.

I CANNOT SIMPLY SWITCH IT OFF, YOU KNOW.

"Now, Vic, I believe you have some information that I am in need of, and I am no longer in a forgiving mood."

And, with that, he charged, not at me, but at my still-prone brother, lying on the ground at the foot of the Tree of Life. Which is how Edik learned what my bad side was really like.

Even I was surprised at how quickly I was able to shift to my dragon form, but only Edik was surprised at how quickly I used those giant jaws to snap down and remove his precariously attached head.

Which I then promptly spat on the ground.

Then I opened my giant maw, and learned that dragon breath gets up to over 900 degrees Celsius in a matter of seconds.

IMPRESSIVE. I DID NOT KNOW YOU COULD DO THAT. DIAMOND IS NOT EASY TO MELT.

"Neither did I," I said, returning to human form and getting thoroughly sick all over the leaves next to the charred remains of what had been Edik's skull less than minute ago.

IF YOU ARE WONDERING, HE IS DEFI-
NITELY DEAD THIS TIME. I AM THE TREE
OF LIFE. I WOULD KNOW.

I laughed, threw up a little more, and said,
"Yeah, Life, I'd guessed as much this time. But
thanks."

And then I passed out.

O NE OF THESE days I was really going to have to get tested for anemia or something. I mean, who passes out this much? Of course, with the number of times I had been healed by the Tree of Life, you would think that I couldn't have any diseases left. Which made one wonder what was wrong with my life, that I kept fainting. Something to think about another time, I guess.

"Is she going to be ok?"

It sounded like it was time to open my eyes.

"There she is," Seamus said, as I blinked him into focus before me.

"Gatita! Nice of you to come back so soon," Sol added, from next to Seamus.

They were sitting on chairs, side by side to the left of the bed I was lying in. Which was a bed I didn't really recognize, though the style of it seemed familiar. When I finally looked at the walls and took a deep breath filled with cool, dusty air, I realized that I recognized where I was.

"We're at Rhelia's house?"

They both nodded.

"Gwen showed up with you, Rhelia, and Trevor a few hours ago, and dropped you here."

"Are they alright?" I asked, my voice cracking even as the words came out.

Sol and Seamus didn't say anything.

"Seamus?"

"He said you killed Rhelia, and… is she really dead? She looked dead."

"It's true. Well, sort of true, I guess. It was true, briefly. Or maybe it was never true. Maybe you can't really ever change the past, I don't know. But, at any rate, as far as he and I were both concerned, there was a brief period of time in which I definitely killed Rhelia."

"I assume it was an accident," Seamus said.

I thought about that for a long moment.

"It was, I guess. The first time, anyway. I mean, I didn't know it was her, but… honestly, even if I'd known, I don't know what I would have done differently. If she'd injected him, we all would have died. Not just us, but a half a million people who had no idea what was going on and just had the bad luck to live in the city that Rebecca Dryer decided to use as a testing site, and…" I trailed off when I saw that both Seamus and Sol were staring fixedly at their hands.

"What is it?" I asked.

"Dryer got away," Sol said.

I looked at them both again.

"That's not all," I prompted, taking in the pallor that tinged both of their faces. "Go on…"

"They… MOME captured Siara and two other weredragons."

"Fuck. Fuck. Fuck. That is sooo not good. So very not good. Where are they? What are we doing to get them back?"

Sol was quiet for a long time, while she stared at the wall. Then she said, "We just got word that she injected one of them in Sucre."

I felt the urge to faint again. To disappear into some kind of void and never return.

"How bad is it?" I whispered.

"It must have been a weaker weredragon… it took out a few city blocks. They're not sure how many people were killed yet. In the thousands, likely. Luckily, Albert says he hasn't detected any tears in spacetime yet."

"Luckily." The word felt so flat in my mouth I wanted to spit it out. Instead, I could feel my stomach start to turn.

"Have we already lost?" I asked, not really expecting an answer. "How do we get them back?"

Sol and Seamus just stared at me. Right. How would they know? And what could I even do?

"Did Gwen say anything about Rhelia?" I asked, needing desperately to cling to the only thing that had gone right so far today. Rhelia and Trev were alive. They had to be. I had done everything I could to save them, and they had to be alright.

"Gwen said she was dead, Vic," Sol said, her own voice cracking.

I swallowed. I didn't think I could handle pretending that it was true with Seamus and Sol. Especially if Trev...

Trev? Trev. I know you can't forgive me, but... will you talk to me? Is... is Rhelia alright?

The silence that followed gutted me a hundred times over. I considered reaching out to Rhelia myself, but something stopped me, maybe just a desperate need to know my brother would still talk to me. Even though it was seeming more and more like he wouldn't.

She's alright, Vic. We won't have to keep this up for much longer. Gwen just said that the more people who thought she was dead the better, and Rhelia agreed.

It felt like a hand had finally stopped squeezing my chest, when I felt Trev through the bond.

All will be well, Living Cat. You should ressssst.

I wanted to ask them both a million questions, not least of which was why we had to pretend Rhelia was dead, but I didn't want to bother them right now, and I wasn't going to argue with them even if rest was the last thing on my mind, and nothing was going to be "well" anytime soon.

There were two weredragons out there who were in desperate need of rescue, not to mention all the people who would die if they were weaponized.

"Rebecca Dryer has declared war against… well, everyone who isn't MOME, really," I said, to no one in particular.

Sol smiled then, and grabbed my hand, and Seamus piled his hand on top.

"Well, she really picked the wrong people to fuck with, didn't she?"

"I DIDN'T EXPECT to see you again," said a south London accent, somewhere behind me.

I jumped nearly a foot in the air. I hadn't expected to find them so easily.

I turned, my vision sweeping past the strange orange sky dotted with purple clouds, lowering to a low grey rock as I took a reluctant breath of sulphur-tinged air. My eyes settled on a small, ugly rodent with red skin and glowing eyes.

"I can see why you wanted to return to Earth so badly," I said, smiling at the small creature, that sat on the low stone in front of me. "But I'm not sure why you came back here so soon after you arrived."

Azrael huffed.

"I wasn't exactly keen on returning here, but it was better than the alternative."

"Which was?" I asked.

"Continuing to spy on you and your mates," they replied.

I wasn't sure if they meant my friends, or my romantic-partners-as-decided-by-Gaia, but since they were largely the same group of people, I decided it didn't matter.

"And sabotage us?" I guessed, thinking of the fire at my old house in Colorado.

Azrael shrugged.

"If necessary. MOME wasn't specific about the particulars, but that angry woman with a stick up her arse wanted to know what you were up to and wanted you out of the way if possible."

"Sounds like Dryer," I said. "So why'd you come back here?"

"I only agreed because she sicced a mob of bloody vampires on me, and threatened to do the same again, if I didn't cooperate."

I considered that.

"Vampires don't seem to pose much trouble for you," I offered.

"Not a lone vampire in the woods who isn't expecting me, no. But a damned bunch of trained ones, yeah. Vampires are—never mind. I don't owe you an explanation."

It was my turn to shrug.

"I suppose not, but I still don't understand why you're here and not on Earth, tailing us and stirring up trouble. Setting houses on fire, or whatever—"

"I didn't—" Azrael let out a long sigh and then started again. "Look. I was fine with the idea of keeping a couple of kids out of Dryer's way, yeah? But I am not interested in blowing up cities full of humans, or stripping people of their dark matter to do it, alright? Dryer crossed the line, and I'd rather starve here in the Wastelands than help with that kind of thing. You may hate me for what I've done already, I wouldn't blame you, but even a succubus has morals."

That made me smile, and I remembered the shadow I had almost followed in the Dragon Realm, just before we'd gone to La Paz the second time.

"Besides," Azrael continued, "I saw what you were doing to help, and I suspect you might be the only thing standing between Dryer and full control of the realms we know."

"Well," I said, reaching out a hand towards the creepy demonic squirrel body that offered such a stark contrast to the angelic forms Azrael could take on Earth, "if that's how you feel about it, I have a proposition for you, Az."

"Oh, and what's that?" The squirrel asked, sniffing my hand skeptically.

"I need help taking down Rebecca Dryer, and everyone who supports her," I said.

"Oh, is that all?" Azrael said, frowning their little squirrel mouth at me.

"That's the short version, yeah."

My hand still lingered in the air between us.

Azrael leapt, clung to my arm, and then ran across my shoulders to perch beside my head.

"Well, go on then."

Vic's adventures continue in *Victoria Marmot Book 4*, coming soon!

The Chronicles of Gensokai Series:
Blade's Edge
Traitor's Hope

Short stories:
Rain on a Summer's Afternoon

Follow Virginia on social media:
www.virginiamcclain.com
twitter.com/gwendamned
facebook.com/virginiamcclainauthor

ACKNOWLEDGEMENTS

These books wouldn't have been possible without a fair bit of help from a number of people. My deepest gratitude goes out to the following people:

My editor, Aurora Wilson-McClain, for not only working with my sometimes ridiculous deadlines, but also for helping me sort out the best use of obscure spell references, the number of "s"s a certain dragon uses in her speech patterns, and where, exactly, everyone has left their clothes.

My husband, for putting up with me disappearing every evening for months on end in order to get these books written, for being my best cheerleader and for not giving me too much grief when I failed to get my half of the housework done.

Cedar, for letting me ignore her often enough to get formatting done, as well as promotion and marketing stuff, and for being so willing to hang out with her wonderful caregivers.

Anne, Lee, Jim, and Gabi, for keeping Cedar entertained, fed, and happy so that I could write.

To my Patreon supporters: Paul, Corey, Mishy, and Jessica.

And finally, the folks at Stella's au CCFM for always putting up with me occupying a table for hours on end while only ordering a cup of tea.

Virginia McClain is an author who masqueraded as a language teacher for a decade or so. When she's not reading or writing she can generally be found playing outside with her four legged adventure buddy and the tiny human she helped to build from scratch. She enjoys climbing to the tops of tall rocks, running through deserts, mountains, and woodlands, and carrying a foldable home on her back whenever she gets a chance. She's also fond of word games, and writing descriptions of herself that are needlessly vague.

For more information check out

www.virginiamcclain.com

facebook.com/virginiamcclainauthor

twitter.com/gwendamned

bookbub.com/author/virginia-mcclain